Enid

CHRISTMAS WISHES

To
CONNOR
HAPPY CHRISTMAS 2020
Love from.
Nana
& PP

h HODDER

D0244604

HODDER CHILDREN'S BOOKS

This collection first published in Great Britain in 2020
by Hodder & Stoughton

1 3 5 7 9 10 8 6 4 2

Enid Blyton ® and Enid Blyton's signature are registered trade marks
of Hodder & Stoughton Limited
Text © 2020 Hodder & Stoughton Limited
Illustrations © 2020 Hodder & Stoughton Limited

A CIP catalogue record for this book is available from the British Library.

ISBN 978 1 444 95719 8

Typeset by Avon DataSet Ltd, Alcester, Warwickshire

Printed and bound in Great Britain by Clays Ltd, Elcograf S.p.A.

The paper and board used in this book are made from
wood from responsible sources.

Hodder Children's Books
An imprint of Hachette Children's Group
Part of Hodder & Stoughton
Carmelite House
50 Victoria Embankment
London EC4Y 0DZ

An Hachette UK Company
www.hachette.co.uk
www.hachettechildrens.co.uk

Contents

The Dog that Hated Christmas

The Dog that Hated Christmas

THERE WAS once a dog who hated Christmas. Now this may seem queer to you, who think Christmas is the jolliest time of the year – but, you see, Rollo, this dog, lived with a dull family who always went away at Christmas time to a hotel.

And the hotel wouldn't take dogs. So poor Rollo was always left behind in the house with the old rather bad-tempered cook. She didn't like Rollo, so she shut him up in an attic with a dish of dry biscuits and a bowl of water all alone. There he stayed, forlorn and miserable, until his family came back.

It was no wonder that he hated Christmas, was it?

As soon as he heard the word, he began to shiver and shake, for nobody but a dog knows how lonely a feeling it is to be shut up all day long and never see a kind face or hear a kind word.

Now there came a time when Rollo's family wanted to move away to another country altogether, and they didn't want to take Rollo. So they gave him to the gardener, who took him home to his cottage and showed him to his children.

There had been no children in Rollo's family, and at first the dog was half scared of the merry shouts and hearty pats he got. But soon he loved it all and made friends with John the boy, Alice the girl and Pip the baby. He loved the children's mother too; she was so plump and kind and gay.

'Rollo! Rollo! Where are you?' shouted the children all day long. 'Come for a walk. Come for a game. Come for your dinner. Rollo! Rollo!'

And Rollo always scampered up, woofing loudly, his tail wagging as fast as a propeller of an aeroplane.

He was as happy as the day is long, and he couldn't help hoping that his first family would not want him back again.

Then one day he heard the word he hated.

'Christmas will soon be here,' said John.

'Oooh, Christmas!' said Alice.

'Ooh!' said the baby, who had only had one Christmas, but thought it must be something lovely.

Rollo put his tail down when he heard the word 'Christmas'. He crept into a corner.

'Gracious! What's the matter with Rollo?' said Alice in surprise. 'Are you ill, Rollo? Have you been naughty? Why do you look so sad and miserable?'

Rollo put his head on his paws and looked at the three children. 'Woof, woof, woof, woof!' he said. That meant, 'Who wouldn't be miserable when Christmas comes? Horrid time of year.' But the children didn't understand at all.

Nearer and nearer Christmas came. Every time Rollo heard people talking about it he shivered and trembled, and thought of being shut up for days alone. And he suddenly made up his mind to run away for Christmas.

Yes, he would run right away, and then nobody could go and leave him shut up in a nasty, musty room without a kind word or pat. He would go to a farm he knew and live in a stable till that horrid Christmas time was over.

So, on Christmas Eve, Rollo crept out of the back door and ran off to the farm nearby. He snuggled himself down in the stable straw, put his head on his paws and thought how he hated Christmas. He didn't think he would find anything to eat for a few days, unless the horses let him share their corn – but never mind, he would have a good meal when he went back.

Rollo slept peacefully on the straw, while the big carthorses snorted and breathed their steamy breath into the air. He awoke early on Christmas morning and remembered where he was. Good! Nobody had shut him up alone *this* Christmas. But, tails and whiskers, how hungry he was!

A horse gave him a few grains of corn. While Rollo was chewing them, a big black cat poked her nose in at the door.

'Oh, there you are, Rollo,' she said. 'Why have you left your nice family? The children are crying because they can't find you.'

'Haven't the family gone away then?' asked Rollo in surprise. 'My first family always did.'

'Of course they haven't,' said the cat. 'Families don't always do the same things. You'd better go back.'

'But if I do, I shall be locked up alone for days,' said Rollo. 'I know all about Christmas, black cat. I've seen five Christmases and they were all as horrid as each other.'

'Well, do as you please,' said the cat, and walked off, her long tail straight up in the air.

Rollo lay and thought for a while, and then he made up his mind that he couldn't bear to think of those children crying for him – he would go back, even if they *did* lock him up for Christmas. So he ran out of the stable and scampered home down the frosty white roads.

The door was shut. He scraped at it with a paw. John opened it – and he gave a great shout.

'Rollo! Dear, dear Rollo! We thought you were lost for ever. Happy Christmas, Rollo.'

He hugged the surprised dog, and then Alice patted him hard, crying, 'Happy Christmas, Rollo darling. Where have you been? We were so miserable without you – but now Christmas will be lovely.'

'Lovely,' said the baby, crawling to Rollo and hanging on to his tail.

'Rollo, here's your Christmas present,' said John, and he gave Rollo the very biggest, juiciest bone he had ever seen.

'And here's what *I've* bought you,' said Alice, and she gave him a bag of his favourite biscuits. 'I bought them with my own money for you because I love you.

You are the dearest dog in the world.'

'Woof! Woof!' said Rollo, and he wanted to cry because he was so surprised and happy.

Then Pip the baby stroked Rollo and gave him a red ball. 'Ball,' said Pip. 'Ball.'

Bones and biscuits, thought the happy dog. *What sort of a Christmas is this? Aren't they going to lock me up alone?*

'Good dog, Rollo,' said the children's mother, and she held out a grand new collar for his neck. 'This is for a good dog. See if it fits him, John.'

It did – and Rollo did look fine. Then the children's father tied a red ribbon to the collar to make Rollo look Christmassy.

'Woof!' said Rollo, wishing he could show himself to the black cat. 'Happy Christmas, everybody. So this is what Christmas is really like – all kindness and love. Ah, I'll never say I hate it again.'

That afternoon he took a few biscuits to the horse who had shared his corn with him.

'Happy Christmas,' he said to the horse. 'Did you

know it was Christmas? Christmas is a lovely time.'

'Ah, you've changed your mind,' said the horse, munching the biscuit. 'Christmas is what people make it, Rollo. Just you tell everybody that, and it will be a wonderful time for grown-ups and children and animals too.'

So Rollo sends you a message, children. He says, 'Make others happy at Christmas and you'll be happy yourself too.'

The Little Fir Tree

The Little Fir Tree

ONCE UPON a time there was a little fir tree not much bigger than you. It grew in a forest on the mountainside. It was an evergreen, so it did not drop all its narrow green leaves in the autumn, but held on to some of them all the year round.

Many little fir trees grew around it. Nearby were some full-grown firs, tall and straight and strong. Sometimes men came to cut them down and to send them away. Then the little fir tree would wonder where they were going, and would feel sad.

'It is dreadful to be cut down,' said the little tree. 'Dreadful to have our branches sawn off, and to be nothing but a straight pole!'

'Do not be sad,' said a big fir tree nearby. 'We are going to be made into straight telegraph poles – and some of us will be the masts of ships. Ah, that's a grand end for a fir tree – to be planted in a ship, and to hold the flapping sails that send the ship along!'

The little fir tree thought that would indeed be a grand life. It hoped that when it had grown tall and straight it too would end as a mast in a ship.

It would be grand to drive along over the water, hearing the wind once again, being of use for many, many years, thought the little fir tree.

All the small growing fir trees hoped the same thing, and they grew a little each year. Then one winter there came a great storm.

It broke on the mountainside where the forest of fir trees grew. It sent a great wind blowing through their branches.

'We shall fall, we shall fall!' said the fir trees, and their branches tossed and shouted in the wind.

'We have no deep roots!' they said. 'Do not blow so hard, wind! You will blow us over!'

'You should grow big deep roots,' said the wind. 'I cannot uproot the strong oak, because it sends its roots deep down. But your roots are too near the surface!'

One big fir tree gave a deep groan. The wind had blown so strongly against it that it was pulled right out of the ground. It toppled over – it fell!

It crashed against the next fir tree and made that fall too. That one fell against a third tree, and down this went as well. Crash! Crash! Crash!

Each falling tree hit the one next to it, and soon many were falling, like a row of dominoes, through the forest. The last one fell on the little fir tree, and pulled it up by its roots.

The gale died down. The sun came out. Men came into the forest to see what trees had been blown down.

'Look – a great path has been made in the forest, by one tree uprooting the next,' said one of the men.

'We will clear away the fallen trees.'

So, very soon, the sound of axes was heard in the forest, and one after another of the fallen trees was chopped away from its roots, its branches trimmed off, and it was taken away to be made into a telegraph pole or the mast of a ship.

The men came to the little fir tree, which had been uprooted by the last falling tree. 'Look,' said one, 'here is a young tree uprooted. It is almost dead.'

'Give it a chance,' said another man. 'We will replant it and see if it will grow.'

So they put the little fir tree back into the ground and stamped down the earth around its roots.

The little tree was almost dead. Its roots were half frozen. It felt ill and weak.

But soon its roots took firm hold of the earth again, and began to feed the tree. It felt better. Its branches stiffened a little. It put its topmost spike straight. All spruce firs have a spear at the top, which they stick straight upwards to the sky. The little fir tree was glad to point its spike up again too.

But, because it had been uprooted for so long, the little fir tree did not grow well. It was short and stunted. It did not grow freely upwards as the other young trees did. It remained small and short, not much bigger than you.

'You must try to grow,' said the other trees. 'If you don't, you will be pulled up and burnt, for you will be of no use to anyone. Try to grow, little fir tree.'

'I am trying,' said the little tree. 'But something has happened to me. I am afraid I shall always be small. I have lost the power of growing.'

It did grow a very little – but by the time the other firs were tall and straight, the little fir tree was very tiny still. It was sad.

'I know I shall be thrown away,' it said to itself. 'I know I shall. I did want to be of some use in the world – but now I shan't be. When the men come to look at the other young trees they will think they are fine – but they are sure to pull me up.'

Sure enough, when the men came round just before Christmas, they were very pleased with the other young firs – but they did not think much of the little one.

'This is a poor tree,' said one. 'It will never be any good.'

They went on into the forest. But later on one of the men came back to the little fir tree. He dug round its roots, and then pulled it out of the ground. He put it over his shoulder.

'Goodbye!' called the little fir tree to all its friends. 'Goodbye! I am going to be thrown away. I am of no use. But I wanted to be; I did want to be!'

The man walked down the mountainside with the little tree. He came to a cosy house, with lights shining from the windows, for it was almost dark. He stamped into the house, shook the snow off his shoulders and called loudly, 'Peter! Ann! I've got something for you!'

Two children came running out, and they shouted

for joy to see the little fir tree. 'Oh, what a dear little tree! It's just the right size!'

Then a good many things happened that puzzled the little fir tree very much. It was put into a big tub. The tub was wound round and round with bright red silk, and looked very gay.

Then clips were put on the branches of the little tree, and candles were stuck into the clips! Soon it had candles from top to bottom!

Then bright, shining ornaments were hung from every branch. Some were blue, some were red, some were green and some were yellow. They were very lovely, made of the finest glass.

'I am beautiful!' said the little tree in surprise. 'I may be small and undergrown – but how lovely I am, dressed in these shining things! How the children must love me!'

Then other things were hung on the little tree – presents wrapped in bright paper. Some of them pulled down the branches, for they were heavy, but the little tree didn't mind. It was too happy to mind anything.

Strings of glittering tinsel were hung everywhere on the tree. And then, at the very top, a wonderful fairy doll was put, with a silver crown and wand, and a fluffy frock that stood out all round her.

'I never saw such a beautiful tree as you!' said the fairy doll. 'Never! I am proud to be at the top of you. You have a nice straight spike there that I can lean against.'

'All spruce firs have those spikes at the top,' said the fir tree proudly. 'That is how you can tell us from other fir trees. Why have the children made me so beautiful, little doll?'

'You are their Christmas tree!' said the doll. 'Didn't you know that children take little fir trees at Christmas time, dress them up and hang their presents there? Ah, it is a wonderful thing to be a Christmas tree, and bring happiness and joy to many people.'

'I am glad I didn't grow,' said the little tree. 'Oh,

I *am* glad I didn't grow. Once I wanted to be the mast of a ship. Now I am glad to be a Christmas tree.'

It shone softly when the candles were lit. 'We have never had such a lovely Christmas tree before,' said Peter. 'Isn't it beautiful? Its branches are just the right size. It is a dear little tree.'

'We will plant it out in the garden when Christmas is over,' said their mother. 'Then it will take root there – and maybe next year we can dig it up again and have it once more for our tree!'

'And the year after – and the year after!' cried the children.

So I expect they will. What a lovely life for the little fir tree – to grow in the wind and the sun all the year, and to be a shining Christmas tree in the winter!

Julia Saves Up

Julia Saves Up

JULIA WONDERED what to give her mother for Christmas. She could ask her what she wanted, of course, but that wouldn't make it a surprise for Mother. And Julia really did want to give her mother a proper surprise present.

She found out quite by accident something that her mother really would like. It was a red and green scarf in the draper's shop! Mother stopped by the shop, looked in and said, 'Oh, what a lovely scarf! Just what I want to go with my new red coat with the green pattern in it! Dear me – it's ten shillings! I can't afford *that* just before Christmas time.'

Julia looked hard at the scarf. She too thought that it was very pretty, and just right for her gay, dark-haired mother. She would look sweet in it, either tied round her neck, or over her curly hair.

And Julia then and there made up her mind that she would most certainly buy that scarf for Mother's Christmas present!

She opened her moneybox when she got home. She had three shillings in it. Oh, dear! That wasn't very much. Could she possibly save seven more shillings before Christmas time? There were other people to buy presents for too – but perhaps she could make the presents, instead of buying them. Yes, she would do that, and spend all her money on her mother.

So she began to save. She had sixpence a week, and each week the sixpence went into her box for Mother's scarf. She earned pennies by running errands, and those went into the box too. Daddy gave her an extra sixpence for cleaning his bicycle. Good! That was another sixpence towards the red and green scarf.

Then Auntie Dora came to stay for two days, and she gave Julia a whole shilling for herself. 'Buy something at the toy shop,' she told Julia.

But Julia didn't. She put it into her moneybox. Soon she had eight shillings! What a lot of money. Only two more shillings were needed and she could go and buy the scarf!

Then Auntie Dora fell ill. 'You must buy her a little bunch of flowers and take them to her,' said Mother. 'You have plenty of money in your moneybox. Buy her a bunch of violets, Julia. There are some in the shops already.'

'But I'm saving up for something, Mother!' said Julia.

'Well, surely you can spare just a shilling for a few flowers for poor Auntie Dora,' said Mother.

'Mother, it's *your* present I'm saving up for,' said Julia. 'It's something special I know you want.'

'But there's nothing special I want,' said Mother, puzzled. 'You haven't even *asked* me what I want!'

'Well, I know, all the same,' said Julia. 'I can't buy flowers for Auntie Dora, Mother.'

'You must,' said Mother, 'even if it means that you can't buy me the present you want to. *I* shan't mind what you give me, dear!'

But Julia minded. She minded very much. She did so badly want to give Mother that scarf. Still, she had to take a shilling from her box and spend it on flowers for Auntie Dora – and then she had only seven shillings.

It's Christmas next week! thought Julia in a panic. *Oh, dear! I shall never, never earn three shillings in time. And that scarf may be sold this week. Somebody else may want to buy it for* their *mother!*

This was a dreadful thought. Julia didn't know what to do. Then she made up her mind.

I'll go to the shop, and ask them if they will let me have the scarf if I pay them seven shillings now and six Saturday sixpences for six weeks after Christmas, she thought. *That's the only way I can do it. Mother would lend me the money, I know – but I simply can't borrow money from her to buy her a present!*

So Julia took her seven shillings and went off to the shop. She went in and spoke to the shopwoman there. 'Please, you have a pretty red and green scarf in the window, and it's ten shillings. I've got seven, and if you'll let me have the scarf for my mother's Christmas present, I'll bring you my Saturday sixpence each Saturday for six weeks.'

'The scarf is sold,' said the shopwoman. 'It was bought about ten minutes ago, miss! What a pity! But even if it hadn't been sold I couldn't have let you have it for seven shillings and the rest paid later. We don't do that sort of thing here.'

Julia was very disappointed. Sold! The scarf she had saved up for and wanted so badly for Mother! It was really too bad.

She felt the tears coming into her eyes and was ashamed to let the shopwoman see them. So she ran out of the shop into the street.

It was a very windy day, and the wind blew Julia's tears away. The little girl went down the street and turned into the lane that went to her home. And, would you believe it, there, lying in the muddy gutter, was a red and green scarf!

Julia couldn't believe her eyes. How had it got there? It must have blown off the neck of the person who had bought it only a little while ago – and she hadn't noticed it.

Julia picked up the scarf. It was muddy, but it could be washed. Suppose – yes, just suppose – she took it home, and washed and ironed it, and gave it to Mother – nobody would ever know. She did so badly want Mother to have that pretty scarf!

'It's for Mother, not for myself,' said Julia. 'It would be dishonest if I took it for myself. But surely it wouldn't be dishonest if I took it for Mother. She wouldn't know I'd found it. And I don't know who it belongs to.'

She set off home with the scarf – but she hadn't

gone very far before she swung round, and walked back down the lane again, her cheeks burning.

'It *would* be dishonest. I know it would. Mother would be dreadfully upset if she knew. And I *can* find out who it belongs to. I can ask at the shop. Oh, how could I ever have thought for a moment that I could pick it up and take it for Mother. I'm horrid, horrid, horrid!'

She went back to the shop. 'Oh, yes,' said the woman. 'It was Mrs Peters who bought it. She lives just down the lane, you know. She *will* be glad to have it.'

Julia hurried off to Mrs Peters' house. She rang the bell. Mrs Peters came to the door.

'Is this your scarf?' asked Julia, holding it out. 'I found it down the lane.'

'Oh, *yes*,' said Mrs Peters, taking it. 'The wind must have blown it off my shoulders. I looked everywhere for it, but I couldn't see it. What a very nice, honest child you are to bring it back to me!'

Julia went red. She remembered how nearly she had taken the scarf home, not meaning to tell anyone she had found it. Then she remembered how badly she had wanted to have it for her mother, and looked suddenly miserable.

'What's the matter, dear?' asked Mrs Peters kindly. 'Are you upset about something? Come inside for a minute and have a biscuit.'

Julia felt herself pushed gently into a room where a big fire was burning. 'Now, you tell me what's the matter,' said Mrs Peters, opening a biscuit tin.

'Nothing much,' said Julia in rather an unsteady voice. 'It was only that – that I had been saving up to buy that scarf for my mother for Christmas – and I'd only got seven shillings – and I went to ask the shopwoman if she'd let me have it for that, and I could pay the rest afterwards – and she told me it had been sold.'

'What a dreadful disappointment for you!' said Mrs Peters. 'And then you suddenly find it in the gutter! I expect you wished you could run off with it, back home!'

'Oh, I did,' said Julia. 'I was horrid for a few minutes and I'm so ashamed. I – I almost did take it back home, Mrs Peters.'

'Well, you needn't worry that *that*,' said Mrs Peters. 'We are all tempted at times, you know, to do horrid things, and we can't help that – but we *can* help saying "No" to the temptation, and that is what you did. It isn't the temptation that matters – it is the saying "No". And you did say "No".'

'Yes, I did. But I'm most dreadfully disappointed about the scarf all the same,' said Julia, feeling much better now.

'Well, I wonder if you'd like to have the scarf for half price,' said Mrs Peters. 'I thought it would go with my red and green dress, but it doesn't. I'd be glad to let you have it for five shillings, if you'd like it.'

'Oh, *no*! Why, you paid *ten* shillings for it only this morning!' cried Julia.

'I know. But since then I've worn it – it's been blown off my neck – it's got muddy and dirty – and it's certainly not worth ten shillings any more. But you could wash it and iron it and make it as good as new, I'm sure. And I'd be pleased to have the five shillings to put towards another scarf,' said Mrs Peters.

Well, what do you think of that? It didn't take Julia long to make up her mind, you may be sure. She paid Mrs Peters the five shillings, took the scarf and said goodbye and thank you very much, and hurried off home.

She washed and ironed the scarf carefully, and it looked as good as new. Julia wrapped it up in gay paper and wrote a label for it: *For my darling mother, with love from Julia.*

And as she had two shillings over after all, she bought Daddy some of his favourite tobacco. He *was* pleased. As for Mother she could hardly believe her eyes when she saw the lovely scarf.

'Just exactly what I wanted!' she said to Julia. 'However did you guess?'

Wasn't it a good thing that Julia took the scarf to Mrs Peters?

Fairy's Love

Fairy's Love

ONCE UPON a time there was a boy called Paul, who was very unhappy. He lived in a tiny cottage with his mother, who was very poor, and his two little sisters. And the reason he was unhappy was because it was Christmas time, when everyone had presents and good things – but there were none for Paul. His mother was too poor.

On Christmas Eve Paul went out to sell wood. He carried a load on his back, and called out 'Wood! Wood!' as he went. Suddenly he came to a house where a party was being held.

'Goodness me!' said Paul, looking into the lit

window. '*There's* a monstrous Christmas tree!'

So there was. It reached right up to the ceiling and glittered and shone like magic. It was hung with goodies and presents, and Paul thought he had never seen anything so fine!

Now as he went on his way he met an old woman, groaning under a load as big as Paul himself carried. In a trice Paul ran up to her.

'Good mother, let me carry it for you,' he said.

The old woman looked at him queerly. 'Carry it up to the top of yonder hill,' she said.

So Paul, puffing and panting, for two loads weighed heavy on his small back, climbed the steep hill right to the top. There he found a small cottage, and the old woman took her load.

'A good deed on Christmas Eve brings fairy's love!' she said. 'Have you a wish to wish, my little friend?'

Paul sighed. 'Wishes aren't any use!' he answered. 'But, oh! Wouldn't I love a Christmas tree of my own!'

The old woman kissed him twice on the forehead, and went inside her cottage. Paul ran down the hill, calling out 'Wood! Wood!' again. But, alas! No one would buy.

Cold and sad, he went home. But look! What was that shining in his little garden? Surely, surely, not a Christmas tree! Paul heard his sisters calling excitedly to him.

'Paul! Oh, Paul! Look and see. Your little dead rose tree has grown candles and goodies, and all *sorts* of presents!'

To Paul's great amazement he saw a beautiful little tree, sparkling and glittering with a hundred candles, and hung with goodies and gay toys!

'Mother! Mother! The fairies have decked my rose tree! There will be presents for all of us!' cried Paul, trembling with excitement. He cut off the gleaming gifts, and gave them to the others. Dolls and books, stockings and sweets, soldiers and trains! A beautiful red shawl for his mother – and what do you think was tucked into a corner of it? Why, a purse full of gold!

When Paul had taken off all the presents they went indoors, for the night was cold. But all night long the little tree twinkled away gaily with its candles and silvery ornaments. The children watched it from the window, while Paul told his mother of the old woman.

In the morning the candles were all gone, and the rose tree stood there alone, bare and brown. But underneath lay a tiny piece of purple paper, and on it was printed very fine and small – *Fairy's love*.

The Cracker Fairies

The Cracker Fairies

ELSIE AND William were so unhappy that they cried streams of tears down their cheeks – and, indeed, it wasn't surprising because they both had bad colds on Christmas Day, and had to stay in bed!

'It *is* bad luck!' said Mummy. 'But it's just no good letting you get up – you might be really ill. So you must play with your presents in bed, and try and be happy.'

But poor Elsie and Will found it very difficult to be happy. Their new toys were on their beds, but they didn't feel like playing with them. They could wind up their new train and new motorcars and bus, but they couldn't let them run on the bed – they got caught in the sheets! So it really wasn't any fun at all.

Mummy was so busy too, because Grannie and Grandpa, Auntie Ellen and Uncle Jim and their children were all coming to tea that afternoon. She had such a lot of things to get ready that she really hadn't had much time for Elsie and William.

'Could John, Joan and Jessie come to see us this afternoon when they come?' asked Elsie.

Mummy shook her head. 'No,' she said. 'You might give them your cold and that would never do. I'm so sorry, darlings, but we will give you a treat when you are better – and you must just be as cheerful as you can without any visitors to see you today.'

Now it so happened that twelve little fairies came by that way, and peeped in at the children's window. When they saw Elsie and William crying they were most surprised.

'Look at that!' said the biggest fairy. 'Crying on Christmas Day! Whatever's happened? Do you suppose they didn't get any presents?'

'They've plenty on their beds,' said the second fairy. 'They must be ill, poor children. What a shame! Let's go and play with them to cheer them up.'

So in at the window they went – but just as they were inside, behind the curtain, the bedroom door opened and the children's mother walked in. The fairies got a terrible fright. Wherever were they to hide?

On the chair nearby was a box of crackers. 'Quick!' whispered the biggest fairy. 'There are twelve crackers, look! We'll each slip inside one, and we won't be seen!'

So into the crackers they crept, right into the very middle, where caps and toys were waiting. They hid there as quiet as mice, and didn't move at all in case the children's mother should see them.

'I wish we could have our crackers now,' said Elsie with a sigh. 'I'm tired of lying here without any excitement at all.'

'Well, you can have them if you like,' said her

mother, and she put the box on the children's bed. 'Now I must go down and see how things are getting on. Be good!'

She went out of the door. Elsie took up a cracker and held it out to Will. 'Pull, Will!' she said. 'We'll see what is inside!'

They pulled hard – BANG! The cracker came in half with a loud pop – and out fell a fairy, a cap and a toy! But the children took no notice of the cap and the toy – they stared in the greatest astonishment and delight at the little fairy with her blue dress and blue wings.

She flew on to Elsie's hand. 'I've come to play with you to cheer you up on Christmas Day,' she said. 'Pull the other crackers, and see what is in them.'

So Will and Elsie pulled a second cracker – BANG! Out fell another fairy, all in pink this time. She flew on to Will's hand and stood there, laughing at him. He was simply delighted.

Well, one after another all those crackers were

pulled, and out fell the twelve fairies, laughing and chattering, flying about the bed and making such a cheerful bird-like noise!

'We'll wind up your toys and set them going on the floor for you to see, if you like,' said the biggest fairy. So down they all flew, and soon the engine, the motorcars and the bus were running busily over the floor. Then the second fairy, who was very good at reading, read a whole story to the children from one of the new books.

By that time it was dinnertime and the children's mother came in with their dinner. The fairies hid under the pillows at once. Mummy was *most* surprised to see the children looking so happy and cheerful!

When they ate their dinner the twelve fairies sat round the edges of the two plates and nibbled crumbs of bread. It was so funny to see them. When Mummy came in again they slipped under the sheet. Elsie nearly laughed out loud because one fairy tickled her leg!

'Now you must have your rest,' said Mummy, and she tucked them up. As soon as she had gone, the fairies slipped out from the bed. 'Where can we have a rest too?' they asked.

'Could you all get into my doll's cot, do you think?' asked Elsie.

They flew over to it. They scrambled in, put their tiny heads on the pillow and were soon just as fast asleep as the two children.

They had tea with the children when they woke up, and when Mummy brought Elsie and William two balloons the fairies played with them all over the room. They flew in the air and bumped the balloons up to the ceiling.

'You are so funny!' laughed Elsie. 'I've never seen anyone play with balloons like that before!'

Then it was time for the fairies to go. They kissed the children, and do you know what two of the fairies gave them – a tiny silver wand each that would do magic!

Mummy found the wands under the pillow. 'I suppose these little things came out of the crackers?' she said. 'What dear little toys!'

'They *did* come out of the crackers!' Elsie whispered to Will. 'They came with the Cracker Fairies!'

The Midnight Goblins

The Midnight Goblins

THERE ONCE lived, many, many years ago, a poor shoemaker and his wife. The man worked very hard at making shoes, but somehow things went wrong for him. People did not pay their bills, his wife fell ill and had to have good food that took all his savings, and altogether the shoemaker was in a very bad way.

At last a day came when he had just enough money to buy the leather to make one more pair of shoes, and that was all.

He bought it and carefully cut out the shoes that evening.

'See, wife,' he said. 'This is my last pair of shoes.

I will sew them up tomorrow, and hope to sell them. If I do not, I cannot tell where the money for our next meal will come from.'

'Poor husband!' said the woman. 'You have worked so hard and so honestly. Surely good luck will come to us, even though this is the very last pair of shoes you have the money to make!'

The man put the cut-out shoes ready on a shelf, thinking to finish them early the next morning. Then he went to bed, and fell sound asleep.

Early next morning he got up, and drew the shutters back to let in the morning sun, so that he could see to finish the shoes. Then he saw something that made him stand still in the greatest astonishment.

There, on the shelf where he had put the cut-out leather the night before, lay a pair of beautiful little shoes! The shoemaker could hardly believe his eyes!

He stared and stared. Then he crossed over to the shelf and picked up the shoes.

'Marvel of marvels!' he cried. 'They are better made

than if I had made them myself! Every stitch is in the right place, and every nail neatly hammered home. This is indeed a mystery! Wife! Wife! What do you make of this?'

His wife was just as astonished as he was.

'It is magic, husband,' she said. 'But it is good magic, so put the shoes in the window and see if you can sell them.'

The man put the shoes in the empty window. Very soon a customer came by and was so pleased with the look of the lovely shoes that he offered the shoemaker twice as much as he expected to get. The cobbler was delighted, and ran in to tell his wife what good luck had come to him.

'There is enough money to buy bread for both of us, and leather for two more pairs of shoes,' said the shoemaker.

He went out to buy the bread, and brought home some more leather. He cut out the two pairs of shoes and laid them on the shelf, ready to begin work early the next morning. Then he went to bed, and he and his wife slept soundly.

The next day he got up and took down the shutters as usual. He turned to look at his bench and – lo and behold! – there was his leather neatly made into two beautiful pairs of shoes again!

'There must surely be magic here!' said the cobbler, very much puzzled. He took the shoes up in his hands, and was delighted to see that they were just as well made as the pair the night before.

He put them in the window at once, and they had not been there five minutes before they were sold, for the passersby thought they looked so comfortable and so well made.

The shoemaker could hardly believe his good luck, for he was paid far more for them than ever he had been paid for shoes before.

'I shall buy meat for us, wife,' he said, 'and I will buy you new ribbons for your bonnet. Even then I shall have enough money left over to pay for the leather for four more pairs of shoes!'

He went out and bought the meat and the ribbons. Out of the new leather he cut four pairs of shoes, and as usual put them up on the bench to finish early next morning.

When he pulled the shutters down he was not surprised to see the four pairs of shoes standing already made on the shelf, stitched as neatly as ever.

He had no difficulty in selling them for a very good price, and this time bought enough leather for eight pairs of shoes. Next morning they were all standing ready for him, and so it went on, night after night, and morning after morning. No matter how many dozens of shoes the shoemaker put out to finish in the morning, they were always ready for him, standing neatly in long rows on his bench. He sold them for a lot of money, and soon became very rich indeed, for the fame of his beautifully made shoes spread far and wide, and folk came from all over the place to buy them. Even the king at last sent for a dozen pairs, and then the shoemaker's fortune was indeed made, for everyone wanted to go to the same shoemaker as the king did.

Now Christmas time came near, and the shoemaker's wife began to wonder if they could do a good turn of some sort to the mysterious helpers.

'Husband,' she said, 'let us sit up tonight to try and find out who it is that comes to help us each night.'

'We will,' said the shoemaker.

So that night the shoemaker and his wife hid themselves behind a curtain in the shop. They left a lit candle on the table, so that they could see who came in, and then they waited patiently until the clock struck twelve.

Immediately the clock tolled twelve, the door of the shop flew open and in skipped two of the funniest little goblins ever seen. They were very tiny, and had hardly any clothes on, so they shivered and shook in the cold December night as they danced about the table and tried to keep themselves warm.

When they had finished dancing about they went to

where the leather lay cut out on the bench, and sat down by it. They sat cross-legged just like the shoemaker did when he sat to make shoes. They threaded their needles and began to stitch. Stitch, stitch, stitch, they went, so fast that the shoemaker could not follow the thread with his eyes. Then they hammered away, and one by one the pairs of shoes were put on the bench, all neatly and prettily made. In the midst of their work the goblins began to shiver so much with the cold that they had to get up and jump about to warm themselves.

The shoemaker and his wife watched in wonder. They could hardly believe their eyes when they saw the shoes being made so quickly. Long before dawn they were all finished, and set out on the bench ready for the shoemaker to find in the morning. Then the goblins jumped down off the table and disappeared out of the door.

'Well, well, well!' cried the shoemaker, as soon as they had gone. 'Did you ever know such kind wee folk as those to come and help a poor man in his trouble like that? I do wish I could do something in return!'

'So you can,' said his wife. 'Did you notice how cold they were? The poor little things had hardly any clothes on! I will tell you what we can do. I will make them each a set of warm clothes, and you can make them a pair of tiny shoes!'

The shoemaker thought that was a very good idea. His wife bought some pieces of scarlet cloth and some lovely soft wool. Then she put on her thimble and began to sew little trousers as neatly as she could. She knitted two little coats as well, and very handsome they looked with tiny green buttons down each side. Then she knitted them the tiniest pair of stockings each, so small that they looked even too small for a doll.

The shoemaker was not idle. He made two pairs of red shoes, the tiniest ones that could be imagined, with little white buttons on each side. He was very proud of them when he had finished, for they were the daintiest and neatest things he had ever made.

When Christmas Eve came the shoemaker did

not put the usual array of cut-out leather shoes on the bench for the goblins to finish, but put instead the two little suits, with the tiny red shoes on top. Then he and his wife hid themselves once more behind the curtain to see what would happen.

Exactly as the clock struck twelve in hopped the two goblins as before, and skipped about to get themselves warm before sitting down to work.

Then they went to the bench to make the shoes. They were struck with astonishment when they saw the little scarlet suits of clothes waiting there for them! They picked them up with many little cries and calls of delight, and then began to dress themselves in them as fast as ever they could. When they came to the red stockings they screamed with joy, and as for the shoes, well, the goblins could hardly get them on, they were so pleased and excited!

When at last they were dressed they danced round and round the shop, singing and shouting for joy, and the shoemaker and his wife were delighted to see that the clothes and shoes fitted the goblins perfectly.

'Smart little goblins now are we,
Dressed in the finest of suits you see,
Never again will we shoemakers be!'

The goblins sang this song again and again as they danced about, and then suddenly rushed out into the night.

They never came back again after that to sew any more shoes for the shoemaker, but he was so rich that he needed no more help, and never lacked for money again.

But the curious thing was that every Christmas Eve after that the two goblins visited the shop to see if there were any new suits for them to replace the old ones that were beginning to wear out. And, of course, the shoemaker and his wife always put some ready, knowing that on Christmas morning they would find them gone.

The Christmas Pony

The Christmas Pony

IT WAS nearly Christmas time. Diana looked at her list of presents. Had she remembered everyone?

'Mummy, Daddy, Auntie, Uncle, Granny, Grandpa, Cook, my teacher, the boy next door, our dog, our cat – and, of course, my darling pony, Nibs!' she said. 'Yes, I've got something for every single one of them.'

She loved Nibs, her pony, very much. He was small, but very strong, and galloped like the wind! She had been saving up for a very long time to buy him a horse rug for Christmas. But still she hadn't nearly enough money.

She was sad about that. *I'll just have to buy him something* small *for Christmas – a bunch of carrots or something*, she thought. *I must keep all the money I've saved for him till I've enough for his rug. Oh, dear – it's such cold weather and I would* like *him to have a rug over him. I'll just have to make do with the old blanket Mummy gave me.*

On Christmas Eve Diana slipped out to the little shed where Nibs was kept. He whinnied when he heard her, and nuzzled into her shoulders. She gave him a hug.

'I've just come to tell you that it's Christmas tomorrow, so I may be a bit late coming to feed you,' she said. 'I'll have my stocking to look at, you see, and presents to undo. I'll bring you a present too.'

She felt about for the blanket. It had slipped off Nibs's back. She pulled it on again. 'It's rather thin and not very warm for you,' she said. 'But one day I do promise I'll buy you a proper rug. Listen for Santa Claus tonight, Nibs – you may hear the bells on his reindeer when he comes driving through the sky!'

Now, it was a most extraordinary thing, but that night Nibs *did* hear bells. Jingle-jingle-jingle! They came nearer and nearer. Jingle-jingle!

They sounded so very near that Nibs really thought they must be in the garden! He looked out through the window into the moonlight.

He saw a strange sight. A large reindeer sleigh was just outside his stable shed, and four big reindeer stood there, tossing their antlers in the moonlit night. A burly man in a long tunic and big black boots and hood got out of the sleigh and went to the front reindeer.

Nibs felt very excited. Good gracious, this must be the person Diana had asked him to watch for! And what were those queer creatures that pulled it? Were they the reindeer? Nibs had no idea what reindeer were. He peered out at the big animals, and admired their great antlers.

He gave a little whinny. He wanted to talk to those

unexpected visitors. One of the reindeer heard him and turned its head. Nibs whinnied more loudly. Then he got so excited that he pawed at his stable door, wishing he could get out. He whinnied very loudly indeed.

Diana, who was asleep in bed, suddenly woke up. She sat up. What had awakened her? Then she heard Nibs's whinnying and was astonished.

What's the matter with him? she thought. *Is he ill? Oh, dear! I do hope not. I'll go and see.*

She slipped on a woolly coat and her warm dressing gown, and put on her slippers. Then she crept downstairs and opened the garden door. She ran across the grass and then behind the hedge where the stable shed was.

She stopped in the greatest astonishment. There, in the moonlight, was the big sleigh and the four reindeer – and, kneeling down by the front reindeer, feeling one of its forelegs, was Santa Claus himself! It must be – he looked *exactly* like his pictures!

Diana stood still with a gasp of surprise and delight. In her garden! Just by Nibs's shed! No wonder he had whinnied and woke her up. What a very extraordinary thing.

'Oh, please,' said Diana with another little gasp, 'is it *really* you, Santa Claus?'

Santa Claus looked up, startled. He hadn't heard Diana coming. He stood up and gave her a very wide smile. Then he patted her curly head.

'Well, well! You're not supposed to see me come along, you know! You're supposed to be fast asleep in bed. Now don't you tell anyone you've seen me!'

'Oh, Santa Claus! I do hope I'm not dreaming,' said Diana earnestly. 'Why have you come down in our garden? I thought you went up on the roof and got down chimneys.'

'So I do,' said Santa Claus. 'But you've got a television aerial up on your roof, and one of my reindeer didn't see it. It's hurt his leg rather badly, I'm afraid. I had to come down into the garden to have a look at it.'

'Oh, dear – I *am* sorry,' said Diana in dismay. 'I just never thought of television aerials getting in your way, Santa Claus.'

'Well, I'm not really quite used to looking out for them yet,' said Santa Claus. 'Sticking up out of the roofs everywhere! I shall really have to be careful. The thing is – I don't believe this reindeer is fit to take on my long journey tonight. He's lame already.'

'Can you get another?' asked Diana anxiously.

'No. I might get one at the zoo, but it's rather far away,' said Santa Claus. 'Well, well – this is a to-do – on Christmas night too, when I've so much to do. I suppose *you* haven't got a tame reindeer, have you? People do have such queer pets nowadays.'

'No, I haven't,' said Diana. And then a perfectly wonderful idea came into her head. 'But, oh, Santa Claus – I've got a pony! He's strong and can gallop as fast as any reindeer. He really can! I'll lend him to you for the night if you like. You can put your hurt reindeer into my pony's stable, where he can have a good rest.'

'Well,' said Santa Claus doubtfully, 'well, I've never thought of using a horse before, I must say. But I don't see why I shouldn't, if he gallops fast. I can rub something on his hooves to make him able to go through the air. That's quite easy. I've a good mind to try him! Have you his harness anywhere about?'

'Oh, yes, yes, in his shed!' cried Diana, wild with excitement. 'Oh, Santa Claus, this is wonderful. What a thrill for Nibs! I'll get him at once.'

She ran to the shed and opened the door. Nibs trotted out at once, excited.

Santa Claus had a look at him and liked him. 'Good, strong little fellow,' he said. 'Beautifully groomed too. You must look after him very well, I think. Come here, Nibs. You're going to help me pull my sleigh!'

Well, it wasn't long before the limping reindeer was put into Nibs's stable, and shut up there to rest, and the little pony was harnessed to the sleigh. Santa Claus fixed bells to his reins, and he jingled as loudly as the reindeer!

He tossed his head and pawed the ground in delight. What an adventure! How he jingled! Where were they all going?

Santa Claus lifted up each little hoof and rubbed something shiny on them all. That was to make Nibs able to gallop through the sky, of course. Then Santa Claus got into his sleigh, leant back on the great sack of toys he had there and cracked his whip.

'I'll put Nibs back into his stable and take out my reindeer when we come back!' he called. 'Thank you very, very much. I'll be sure to fill your stocking full of my very nicest toys!'

And then – jingle-jingle-jingle – the reindeer and the dear little pony sprang suddenly into the air, the sleigh tilted up with a jerk, and off they all went at top speed high up over the roofs of all the houses nearby.

Diana blinked in amazement. Why, this was better

than anything she had ever read in a book – much, much more exciting! Nibs, her own pony Nibs, was helping the reindeer to pull Santa Claus's sleigh! Nobody would believe her if she told them. She could hardly believe it herself!

She peeped into the stable and saw the reindeer standing quietly there, his hurt leg lifted up like a dog's lame leg. He shivered a little. Diana put the old blanket over him, and stroked his long, velvety nose. 'You're all right,' she said. 'Keep quiet and rest, reindeer.'

Then she slipped back to bed. She couldn't go to sleep for a very long time. She was listening and listening for Santa Claus to come back with Nibs.

But he didn't come, and at last she fell asleep. She remembered her night adventure immediately when she awoke in the morning, and her eyes shone. She looked at her stocking. It was full from top to toe.

Santa Claus had been down *her* chimney, that was certain! But had she dreamt all that about the hurt reindeer and Nibs taking his place? It didn't seem that it could possibly be true now that it was day – surely things like that didn't really happen?

'I think I must have dreamt it all,' said Diana with a sigh. 'Anyway, I shall never know if it was true, because the reindeer will be gone from the stable this morning, and Nibs will be back in his place – and *he* can't tell me if it was all true or not!'

She decided that she must have been dreaming. It was a pity, but it simply *must* have been a dream. Nibs couldn't go galloping through the sky.

She had a lovely lot of presents, and a very happy Christmas breakfast with more parcels by her plate. Then she got up and fetched her coat.

'I'm just going to see Nibs,' she said. 'I want to give him his carrots and wish him a happy Christmas.'

Out she went and ran to the stable shed. Nibs was there, waiting for her.

He whinnied in delight when he saw the carrots.

'Nibs,' began Diana, 'I wish you a very . . . oh, *Nibs*! *Where* did you get that wonderful horse rug?'

Nibs whinnied. On his back was a magnificent navy blue rug, bound with red. It was thick and warm. On the middle of it were embroidered two gold letters – *S. C.*

'S. C.!' said Diana. 'Santa Claus. They are his initials! Oh my goodness – he must have given you his rug to keep you warm after your long gallop, Nibs. You must have come in very hot, and he didn't think that your thin old blanket was warm enough for you. *Oh, Nibs!*'

Nibs whinnied and nuzzled into Diana's neck. He had had a wonderful adventure. The reindeer had been very, very nice to him. Santa Claus had told him he was just as fast as they were – and he had given him his own rug to keep him warm. What more could a horse want – except a bunch of nice munchy, crunchy carrots to eat on a Christmas morning?

Diana brushed against Nibs's reins, that were hanging nearby. They made a noise – jingle-jingle! The little girl stared in delight.

'Oh! Santa Claus forgot to take off the bells, Nibs! He's left them on your reins. And *I* shan't take them off either. You shall jingle whenever you go out with me!'

So it wasn't a dream after all. It was all true. Diana was so excited and happy that she hardly knew what to do. She stroked the gold initials on the rug. S. C. for Santa Claus. It really was very marvellous.

She went back to the house at last, half wondering if she was *still* dreaming. She looked up at the roof. What a surprise! The television aerial was knocked crooked!

It was done when the reindeer caught his leg on it, thought Diana. *Well, certainly I'm not dreaming. But would anyone believe me if I told them? No, they wouldn't. So I shan't say a word. Nobody shall ever know!*

Well, I simply had to tell *you*, because it's much too nice a story never to be told, isn't it? And if Diana reads it, she won't mind – she'll feel so very, very proud of Nibs!

The Snowman in
Boots

The Snowman in Boots

'HARRY, LET'S build a snowman who really looks alive!' said Valerie.

'We can't,' said Harry. 'They always look so queer about the feet, because they have to be made of snow right down to the bottom, or they wouldn't stand up.'

'Well, I know what we can do,' said Valerie. 'We can get Daddy's old rubber boots, the ones he never wears now because they've got holes in – and we can fill them with snow, and then build the snowman on top of the big boots! It will look exactly as if he has got proper legs in the boots!'

'All right,' said Harry. 'It's rather a good idea.'

So they began to build a snowman. First of all, they got the old rubber boots – they were so big that Valerie could put both her feet inside one of them! Then they stood the boots on the snowy lawn and filled them with snow.

'There,' said Valerie, pleased. 'He's got two snow feet in the boots, and two fine fat legs.'

Then they built a nice round body on top of the boots, and put a round snow head on top. Harry made some arms down by the side of the body.

'Now we'll dress him,' said Valerie. 'I'll get Daddy's old mackintosh from the shed. You fetch that torn red scarf of yours, Harry, and Grandpa's big old gloves, and I'll get the funny old check cap we used for our guy on Firework Night.'

It wasn't long before the snowman was dressed up very well indeed. The mackintosh was draped round his shoulders and came right down to his knees, just above the boots. The scarf was tied round his rather fat throat. The gloves were pinned to the end of the mackintosh sleeves, filled with snow so that they looked like hands.

And then the cap was put on his round head to give him the finishing touch. He *did* look fine!

'A stick now,' said Harry, pleased. 'I'll lend him the one I had for my birthday. He'll like that.'

'And, oh, Harry – let's give him a nice big nose and I'll lend him that pair of glasses I got out of a cracker!' cried Valerie. 'He *will* look real with glasses!'

Well, the children gave him a big nose, a mouth made of twigs, and then set the glasses on his nose. They were quite startled when they looked at him.

'Good morning, Mr Frosty-Man,' said Valerie, bowing. 'I hope you are well!'

'I almost expected him to bow back to you, and take off his cap,' said Harry with a laugh. 'Mother! Come and see Mr Frosty-Man!'

'Who?' cried Mother, looking out of the window. 'Dear me – a visitor – who can it be?'

But it wasn't a visitor, of course – it was only the

funny old snowman with his cap and glasses and coat and big rubber boots!

Everyone stared at him in surprise when they came by. 'Who's that?' said short-sighted Miss Spink. 'Is that Valerie's grandpa? I really must say "How do you do" to him.'

'No, dear, no,' said her sister. 'It's just a snowman!'

The children were quite sad to have to go to bed and say goodnight to the snowman out of the window. He stood there in the snowy night, looking more real than ever now that it was dark. There was just a little moon, enough to show him there.

Now, in the middle of the night, two burglars came along. They meant to break into the shed at the back of the children's house and steal the bicycles there. There were three – one belonging to Valerie, one to Harry, and one to their father.

The men crept in at a gate right at the bottom of the garden. The snowman was in the front garden, so they didn't see him. They went quietly to the shed where the bicycles were kept.

Nearby was a coke bunker, and hiding inside was Paddy-Paws, the children's cat. He was sometimes naughty and wouldn't go in at night. Then he would creep into the coke bunker and sleep there. He awoke when he heard the men whispering, and poked his black head outside.

Hallo! Who are these men? What are they doing to our shed? thought Paddy-Paws. *I must go and warn the family.*

But nobody heard him scratching at the door, so nobody came to see what was the matter. He ran round into the front garden – and there he saw the snowman.

Ah – the snowman! he thought. *Perhaps* he *can help.* So up he went and tapped the snowman on the leg.

'Mr Frosty-Man,' he said, 'will you please come round to the back garden and frighten away two men who are there?'

The snowman was most surprised. 'I can't walk,'

he said in a cold, snowy sort of voice. 'Snowmen never can!'

'Why can't you?' said Paddy-Paws. 'You're wearing boots, and that means you've got feet, and feet can walk, can't they? Why don't you try?'

'Well, I will,' said the snowman, thinking that Paddy-Paws might be right. So he tried to lift up one foot. But it was very, very heavy.

He groaned. 'I don't know how to walk,' he said. 'My legs feel heavy.'

'Oh, do try again,' begged Paddy-Paws. 'Let me loosen the snow round your feet, Mr Frosty-Man. There – can you move them now?'

'Ah, that's better,' said the snowman, and he managed to lift up one foot. He put it in front of him.

'Now you move the other foot,' said the cat. 'That's right. Put it in front of the first foot. Now put the first foot in front again. Oh, you're getting on well, snowman!'

'Thank you for telling me how to walk,' said

the snowman, and he went slowly and heavily over the lawn, on to the path and up to the back gate. Paddy-Paws pushed it open for him and he went through.

He came to the bicycle shed. 'I'm going to make a terrible noise now to frighten the men,' said the cat. 'So don't be afraid. You walk up to them as I yowl.'

Paddy-Paws yowled and howled and wailed and squealed. The snowman suddenly appeared at the door of the bicycle shed just as the men came to see what the dreadful noise was.

'Hey, who's there?' said one man, startled. 'Here, Jim, let's run. Quick!'

Mr Frosty-Man stood there, very big and very fat. The moonlight glinted on his glasses. He raised one arm stiffly, with the stick in it.

'Run, Jim, run!' cried the frightened man, watching. 'Oh, who is it? Oh, that dreadful noise!'

The snowman placed himself right in the doorway, and the men had to pummel him to get out. They squeezed by him at last, and raced to the back gate, leaving all the bicycles behind.

'Good old Mr Frosty-Man,' said Paddy-Paws. 'You scared them all right. Now, shall I help you back to the front lawn again?'

But poor old Frosty-Man had got one of his legs caught in the shed door and he couldn't move, no matter how the cat shoved and pushed. So in the end he had to stay there.

And in the morning how astonished the two children were, when they went to get their bicycles!

'Mother! Mother, look where the snowman has got to!' cried Valerie. 'Who put him at the door of our shed? And, Mother, look at these footsteps going up and down the garden from the gate to the shed!'

'Burglars must have come to get your bicycles, I should think,' said Mother. 'But *how* did the snowman come to be in the doorway of the shed? He couldn't possibly have got there himself. It's a mystery.'

'He must have been able to walk because we gave him boots,' said Harry. 'Didn't you, Mr Frosty-Man? Mother, he winked at me through his glasses, I saw him! He *did* walk here himself, I know he did.'

Well, he did, of course – and a very good thing too. You'd better give your next snowman some boots too. He might find them as useful as Mr Frosty-Man did!

Nid-Nod's Mistake

Nid-Nod's Mistake

IT WAS wintertime, and at Dame Twinkle's school all the little pupils were getting excited about Christmas.

'I am making a pincushion for my mother,' said little Feefo.

'And I am making a pipe rack for my father,' said the brownie who was head of the class.

'Dame Twinkle! Are we going to have a concert?' cried little Pippin. 'Oh, do let's!'

'Of course,' said Dame Twinkle. 'You will be able to sing some of your songs and say some of the nice poems you have learnt. Of course we will have a concert.'

'Oh, Dame Twinkle, we shall be able to decorate the schoolroom well, shan't we?' said Nid-Nod. 'Oh, let's make it really beautiful, shall we?'

'Yes, we will,' said Dame Twinkle. 'We will go out to the woods and fields and fetch in all kinds of nice leaves and berries for decoration.'

'I shall thread holly berries and leaves in a long string and loop it round the lamp!' said Feefo. 'I know how to do that.'

'I shall bring pine branches and stand them in vases in the corners of the room,' said Pippin.

'Pooh! Why bring dull pine branches full of nasty sharp needles?' said Nid-Nod. 'Why not bring some really pretty boughs? I think I shall bring in oak boughs. I do think their leaves are so pretty. They are shaped like feathers.'

Everyone stared at Nid-Nod and laughed. He didn't know why. He glared round at them. Everyone was always laughing at him.

'Laugh if you like,' he said, 'but I tell you oak

leaves are very pretty. Yes, and I shall go and bring in some chestnut leaves too. I love the way they spread out their big finger leaves. I shall put them round the pictures.'

Everyone laughed again.

'Now, now,' said Dame Twinkle with a very bright twinkle in her eye. 'No more laughing and chattering. Soon we will make a list of things for Christmas decorations, and you shall each bring something.'

So, two weeks before the concert, the list was made. Everyone said what he or she would like to bring.

'Holly berries and leaves,' said Feefo.

'I'll bring pine branches,' said Pippin.

'And I'll bring oak leaves,' said Nid-Nod.

Feefo giggled.

Dame Twinkle wrote everything down. *Oak leaves from Nid-Nod*, she wrote. Then she looked at the brownie.

'What will you bring, brownie?' she asked.

'Ivy,' said the brownie. 'I pass plenty on my way to school. I think the leaves are so well shaped, Dame

Twinkle. Some of them are dusty, but I can wash them and dry them and even polish them, can't I?'

'Certainly,' said Dame Twinkle, and she wrote down *Ivy leaves from the brownie*.

'I'll bring some dark green laurel,' said Jinky.

'What, that nasty dark stuff!' said Nid-Nod. 'What dull trees and leaves you are all choosing. Dame Twinkle, I'll bring sprays of pretty birch leaves. They are so small and dainty – much better than the tough, leathery laurel leaves!'

'Very well, Nid-Nod,' said Dame Twinkle, and wrote *Birch leaves* beside Nid-Nod's name too.

'I'll bring some yew from the churchyard,' said Feefo.

'And I'll bring the Christmas tree!' said Dame Twinkle. 'I have a dear little fir tree growing in my garden that will do beautifully for a Christmas tree. They are always spruce fir trees, you know.'

'Good!' said Pippin. 'Now we're all bringing something!'

'I'm bringing the most!' said Nid-Nod proudly. 'And I'm bringing the prettiest leaves too – the oak leaves, the chestnut leaves and the birch leaves. Much nicer than prickly holly and ugly laurel!'

'You won't bring anything, Nid-Nod,' said Feefo with a giggle.

Dame Twinkle rapped on her desk. 'No talking now,' she said. 'Let Nid-Nod bring the things he wants to – and if he does we will be very grateful to him.'

Well, in two or three days the school children began to look for the things they said they would bring. Feefo found plenty of holly leaves and berries and began to string them together very clearly. She found some yew too, with its waxen pink berries.

The brownie brought sprigs of ivy, and washed, dried and polished each leaf till it shone.

Jinky brought branches of dark green laurel, and Pippin brought fine pine branches full of needle-like leaves that pricked quite sharply.

Dame Twinkle dug up the fir tree in her garden and

set it in a pot. It looked lovely. The children longed to see it all dressed up in candles, ornaments and presents.

And about what Nid-Nod? Well, he had promised to bring many things too. 'Oak leaves,' said Nid-Nod. 'I will get those first. I know where the big oak trees grow in the middle of the wood.'

So he went to the wood and found the oak trees. But, oh, dear, what a pity, the one he went to had only a few brown leaves on that rustled and shook in the wind. It had no green ones on at all.

'Bother!' said Nid-Nod. 'I must find another oak tree, I suppose.'

So he went to another one – but that had no leaves on at all! Its branches spread out bare and brown. Nid-Nod scratched his head. 'What a nuisance! I see that all the oak trees are bare. Now, why didn't I think of that? I didn't remember that they dropped their leaves in the autumn.'

He went to where the big, tall chestnut grew, its branches spreading wide on every side. He looked up to find some leaves. But there were no leaves there. Not one of the pretty fan-shaped cluster of leaves was to be seen. The tree was bare, except for its brown buds, already growing fat.

'Well, well, well – so the chestnut tree has dropped its leaves too!' said Nid-Nod, feeling cross. 'How annoying! Why didn't I remember that? Well, I expect the other children too will find they can't bring some of the leaves they said they would. I shan't be the only one!'

He went to find a silver birch tree. He saw the pretty silvery white trunk shining between the trees and ran to it.

But, alas – the birch tree too was bare! Nid-Nod could pick no leaves from it, for the birch tree had thrown them all down in the autumn. There she stood, her fine thin branches waving gently round her like a mist of brown – but not a leaf was to be seen!

'Then I must bring something else, I suppose,' said Nid-Nod, feeling cross with himself. He looked around the woods. What should he bring?

He couldn't bring pine branches because Pippin had chosen those. He couldn't bring yew or holly because Feefo had said she would bring them. He couldn't bring ivy because the brownie was bringing it.

'I can't bring anything! All the others have chosen the things I could bring!' said Nid-Nod, and he began to cry.

Next morning all the children except Nid-Nod had brought their Christmas decorations. Only Nid-Nod's hands were empty.

Dame Twinkle looked at him. 'Where are the oak leaves, the chestnut leaves and the birch leaves you said you would bring, Nid-Nod?' she asked.

'They've all dropped their leaves,' said Nid-Nod gloomily. 'I was silly. I forgot that only evergreens kept their leaves on in the wintertime. I suppose that's why they have such tough, leathery sort of leaves – they have got to last for much longer than a year.'

'Poor Nid-Nod!' said Dame Twinkle as everyone

began to laugh at him. 'So you are the only one left out of the Christmas decorations! Go out into the garden and see if you can find something green to bring in. There may be an evergreen there we have forgotten to use!'

So Nid-Nod went into the garden – and he saw the hedge of green privet that ran round the beds! 'Oh, good!' said Nid-Nod, and he picked some sprays. 'I don't like you very much, privet – but at least you are green in the wintertime, and will give me something to take for the Christmas decorations!'

So Nid-Nod brought some green leaves after all, and decorated the school clock very nicely with sprays of privet. I do wonder what *you* would have chosen to bring, if you had belonged to Dame Twinkle's school! You wouldn't have made a mistake like Nid-Nod, I am sure!

The Empty Doll's House

The Empty Doll's House

SALLY HAD a lovely little doll's house on Christmas Day. She looked at it standing there at the foot of her bed. It had a little blue front door with a tiny knocker that really knocked, and it had four small windows, with tiny lace curtains at each!

'Oh, it's lovely!' said Sally. 'Won't my little Belinda Jane love to live there! She is small enough to fit it properly.'

But when she opened the front of the doll's house Sally got rather a shock. It was empty. There was no furniture in it at all!

She was disappointed. A doll's house can't be

played with unless it has furniture inside, and Sally badly wanted to play with it.

Also, Belinda Jane couldn't possibly live there if it was empty. She must at least have a bed to sleep in, a chair to sit on and a table to have meals on.

She showed the house to Belinda Jane. Belinda looked sad when she saw that it was empty.

'Never mind. I'll save up my money and buy some furniture,' said Sally. 'Maybe I'll get some money today for a present.'

But she didn't. All her aunts and uncles gave her Christmas presents of toys and books, and nobody gave her any money at all.

It was Granny who had given her the dear little doll's house. When she came to share Christmas dinner she spoke to Sally about the house.

'I didn't put any furniture in it, dear,' she said, 'because I thought you would find it more fun to buy some yourself and furnish it bit by bit.'

'Yes. It *will* be fun to do that,' said Sally. 'Only it

will take such a long time, Granny, because I spent all my money on Christmas presents, and I only get sixpence a week, you know.'

When Sally got her first sixpence she went to the toy shop and looked at the doll's furniture there. She saw a cardboard box, and in it was a dear little bed that would just fit Belinda Jane, two chairs, a table and a wardrobe! Think of that!

But, oh, dear, it cost three shillings and sixpence, and there was nothing for one sixpence to buy at all. Sally ran home almost in tears.

'Now, don't be a baby,' said Mummy. 'Everything comes to those who wait patiently. Don't get cross and upset if you can't have what you want. It will come!'

Sally was not a very patient person, and she hated waiting for things she badly wanted. But she always believed what Mummy said, so she went up to the nursery and told Belinda Jane they must both be patient, and maybe they would get the furniture somehow in the end.

Sally was excited the next day, because she was going to a party – and there was to be a Christmas tree. It was sure to be a nice big one, with a present for everyone. And there would be games and balloons and crackers and ice creams. Lovely!

She went to the party in her best blue frock. 'Hallo, Sally!' cried Eileen, dancing up to her. 'There's going to be a prize for every game, did you know? And it's to be money! I do hope I win a prize, because it's Mother's birthday next week, and I want to buy her some flowers.'

Sally was pleased to hear about the prizes too. If only she could win some of the money! She would be able to buy some furniture for Belinda Jane.

They played musical chairs – but Sally didn't win because a rough little boy pushed her out of her chair, and she didn't like to push back.

They played hunt the thimble, but somehow Sally never could see the thimble first! And when they played spin the tray she couldn't get there before the little spinning tray had fallen over flat! So she didn't win any prize at all.

'Now, I mustn't get cross or upset,' she said to herself. 'I mustn't. I must be patient. But I've missed my chance. What a pity!'

After tea the children were taken into another room – and there was the Christmas tree, reaching up to the ceiling, hung with presents from top to bottom.

Just about the middle of the tree there hung a cardboard box – the cardboard box of furniture that Sally had seen in the toy shop! Her heart jumped for joy. Now surely her patience would have its reward – surely she would get that lovely box of doll's furniture!

She could hardly wait for the presents to be given out. She had good manners, so she didn't like to ask for the box of furniture. She just stood nearby, hoping it would be hers.

But to her very great disappointment it wasn't given to her! She was handed a box with tiny motorcars in instead. Sally could have cried! She said, 'Thank you,' and went to a corner, trying not to feel upset.

I wanted to win a prize and I didn't. And I wanted to have the furniture off the tree and I didn't, she thought. *What's the good of being patient? I don't get what I want, however good and patient I am. I feel like shouting and stamping!*

But she didn't shout or stamp, of course, because she knew better. She just sat and looked at the little motorcars, and didn't like them a bit.

A small girl called Fanny came up to her. She held the box of furniture in her hand. She sat down beside Sally and looked at the tiny motorcars.

'Oh, aren't they lovely?' she said. 'I do like them so much. I got this doll's furniture, look. Isn't it silly?'

'Well, I think it's lovely,' said Sally. 'How *can* you think it's silly?'

'It's silly for me, because I haven't got a doll's house,' said Fanny. 'But I *have* got a toy garage! I had it for Christmas. It's only got one car in, and

I do want some more. That's why I like your present and hate mine!'

'Well, *I* had a doll's house for Christmas without any furniture – and I haven't got a garage!' said Sally, her face very bright. 'Can't you give me the furniture and I'll give you the motorcars? We could ask Eileen's mother and see if she minds. It was she who bought all the presents for us.'

They ran to Eileen's mother and told her. She smiled at them. 'Of course, change your presents if you want to,' she said. 'I think it would be most sensible of you. I should have given *you* the furniture, Sally, and *you* the cars, Fanny, if I'd known about the doll's house and the garage.'

The little girls were so pleased. Fanny took her cars home to her toy garage and Sally flew home with her doll's furniture. It went into the doll's house and looked most beautiful!

'There you are, Belinda Jane,' said Sally to her smallest doll. 'Now you can move in. You've got a bed to sleep in, chairs to sit on, a wardrobe for your clothes and a table to have meals on. And I'll buy you a little cooking stove as soon as ever I can.'

Belinda Jane was pleased. She looked sweet sitting on one of the chairs, and even sweeter tucked up in the little bed.

Mummy came to look. Sally gave her a hug. 'Mummy, you were right about waiting patiently. I kept *on* being disappointed, but I wouldn't get cross or upset – and then suddenly the furniture just came to me. Wasn't it lucky?'

'It was,' said Mummy. 'Now, tomorrow I'll give you some old bits and pieces and you can make carpets for Belinda Jane. She will like that.'

You should see Sally's doll's house now. She saved up her money and bought a little lamp, a cooking stove, another bed, a cupboard for the kitchen, two more chairs and a washstand. I really wouldn't mind living in that doll's house myself!

Grandpa Twinkle

Grandpa Twinkle

IN LEMON Village there lives an old man called Grandpa Twinkle. His eyes are very twinkly, that's why he has his name. At Christmas he goes to stay with his two little grandchildren, Mary and Joe – but they are always sad, because Grandpa Twinkle doesn't believe in Santa Claus.

'Stuff and nonsense! Rubbish and fiddlesticks!' Grandpa Twinkle would cry every time Mary said something about Santa Claus. But listen to what happened to him last Christmas Eve!

Grandpa Twinkle went to bed and fell asleep. He awakened by the sound of something falling – plop!

– into his room. He sat up and lit his candle. Something else fell – plop! It was a red ball! It bounced on the rug and then ran under the bed to join the first ball. Grandpa was most astonished.

Then something else fell with a clang into the fireplace. Grandpa looked – it was a small clockwork train! 'Most peculiar!' said Grandpa, and he got out of bed. A doll fell down on to the rug and said, 'Ma-Ma!' Grandpa felt scared and hopped back into bed. But the doll didn't do anything else.

'What a peculiar dream I am having!' said Grandpa Twinkle. 'Whatever will happen next?'

Well, he hadn't long to wait. A wooden horse, a spinning top, another doll, a game of ludo, some soldiers and a book fell in a heap down the chimney! And then down came two large black boots, a red cloak – and Santa Claus inside them!

'Oh, hallo!' he said to Grandpa. 'Sorry to disturb you. My sack's got a hole in it, I'm afraid, and some of the things have been falling out.'

'Don't mention it,' said Grandpa. 'I don't believe in you, so I know you're only a dream! Ha, ha!'

'Ha, ha to you!' said Santa Claus, beaming. 'Well, you might help me to pick up a few of these toys. They are for Mary and Joe. Nice children, those.'

'Very,' said Grandpa, and he began to help Santa Claus to pick up all the fallen toys.

'I think we've got them all now,' said Santa. 'Many thanks. Oh – wait a bit – where's that red ball?'

They couldn't find it, so Santa said it didn't matter. He hoisted his sack on his shoulder, borrowed a safety pin from Grandpa to pin up the hole and crept away to Mary's bedroom to fill her stocking.

'I had to come down your chimney because there isn't one in Mary's room,' he whispered to Grandpa as he went. 'Goodnight. Sleep well!'

'I *am* sleeping well, thank you,' said Grandpa solemnly. 'I know this is a dream. I tell you, I don't believe in you, Santa!'

Grandpa thought no more about it, but snuggled

into bed, and was soon fast asleep. In the morning he awoke and remembered that he had presents to give the two children. So out he hopped and felt under the bed for his slippers. And his hand closed on something round! He pulled it out – it was the red ball that Santa hadn't been able to find the night before!

'But it was a dream!' cried Grandpa. 'I don't believe in Santa!' He ran to ask Mary and Joe what they thought. I expect you can guess what *they* said!

The Stolen Reindeer

The Stolen Reindeer

SANTA CLAUS drove up to Toyland a week before Christmas.

'Whoa! Whoa!' he cried to his eight great reindeer as they arrived at the gates.

The gates slowly opened, and a crowd of gnomes and fairies rushed out.

'Welcome! Welcome! Santa Claus!' they cried, crowding round the big jolly man dressed in a red coat.

'Glad to see you all again!' beamed Santa Claus. 'Now, just get out of the way a bit, and let me drive my reindeer through the gates into Toyland!'

The crowd ran back, and Santa Claus drove straight

through the gates, which shut after him. With fairies and gnomes hanging on to his sledge he drove down the queer higgledy-piggledy streets of Toyland.

'Here we are!' he cried at last as he arrived in front of a large house, which looked really rather like a very smart doll's house. On the steps stood the mayor of Toyland, a little gnome, dressed in a flowing cloak of yellow.

'Welcome, Santa Claus!' called the mayor, going down the steps to greet his visitor, and nearly tumbling over his long cloak. 'We are very glad to see you here again. I hope all the orders you gave us for toys and games have been carried out in a satisfactory manner!'

'I hope so too,' answered Santa Claus, getting out of the sledge. 'I've got just a week to go round Toyland and collect all the toys before I start off on Christmas Eve to deliver them to the children!'

He went into the mayor's house and the mayor gave him an excellent dinner, for Santa Claus had driven many, many miles over the snow.

'Splendid!' said Santa Claus when he had finished. 'Now will you kindly give me the list of orders I sent you, and I will start on my journey round Toyland.'

The mayor took a very long piece of paper from a locked drawer and gave it to Santa Claus.

'Hmm, let me see. The blue fairies are dressing all the dolls this year. I must see if they are ready. The pink fairies are furnishing all the doll's houses. The water pixies are doing all the ships and boats; they ought to be well done this year!'

'I think you will find most of the things are ready for you to take,' said the mayor, looking over Santa Claus's shoulder.

'The gnomes are making the soldiers and forts,' went on Santa Claus, glancing down the paper, 'and the wise elf is looking after the book department and the games. What are the red goblins doing?'

'They are making boxes of crackers for the children to pull on Christmas Day, and when they have parties,' said the mayor. 'I haven't heard anything of them for some time, but I hope they are getting on all right.'

'Well, I'll visit the blue fairies first,' said Santa Claus, getting up from his armchair. 'I'll drive round in my sledge, and put the toys in as I go round for them.'

He jumped into his sledge, shook the reins and drove off to the blue fairies. They lived in the centre of Toyland, in a number of tiny little houses. When they heard his sleigh bells they rushed out.

'Hurray! Hurray!' they cried. 'Here's Santa Claus at last! Come and see all the dolls we've got!' And they dragged him laughingly into the middle house.

In the dining room were all sizes and shapes of dolls. They were sitting in chairs, standing up or leaning against the wall. Some were grown-up dolls, some were dressed like boys and girls, and all of them looked spick and span and beautiful.

'Excellent!' cried Santa Claus. 'You *have* worked hard. But where are the baby dolls? We *must* have baby dolls, you know!'

The blue fairies took him upstairs and there, cuddled in little beds, were the baby dolls, some in long clothes, and some in short baby dresses.

'Sh,' whispered the fairies, 'they're all asleep! Aren't they sweet?'

'They're lovely,' answered Santa Claus, 'and the children will love them, I know. But you can wake them up, and get all of them ready to go in my sledge for me! I want to take them now.'

'Oh, yes, certainly,' said the blue fairies, and they quickly gathered all the lovely dolls from downstairs and upstairs, and soon Santa Claus had them packed safely and comfortably in his big sledge.

'Goodbye!' he called to the fairies as his reindeer started off. 'Goodbye and thank you! You've done very well this year!'

Santa Claus then drove to the water pixies and they were so busy that they didn't hear him coming.

'Goodness me! They *are* busy!' said Santa Claus to himself as he watched the pixies. They lived in a large blue lake on which were growing great white and yellow water lilies, and on the flat lily leaves were their houses.

The pixies were sailing a large fleet of ships, boats and steamers.

'Hi! Look out!' called a pixie. 'Your boat's going to bump into mine!' And he plunged into the water and twisted the boats in different directions.

'They sail beautifully!' cried another pixie. 'Won't the children be pleased with them!'

A tiny little pixie appeared at the door of a house, carrying a submarine.

'Look what I've just finished making!' he cried. 'See if it goes well in the water!' And he launched it from his lily leaf.

'Splendid! Splendid!' cried Santa Claus and all the pixies as they watched the submarine chugging through the water.

'Here's Santa Claus! Hurray!' shouted the pixies, scrambling out of the water to greet him.

'Your boats are fine!' said Santa Claus, smiling. 'Are they ready to be packed into my sledge?'

'Yes, we've just finished them all!' said the pixies, swimming after the floating fleet of ships.

'I'm very pleased with you,' beamed Santa Claus, when the ships were all neatly packed in the sledge. 'I'm going off to the wise elf now for books and games. Goodbye!' And off he went.

The wise elf was very pleased to see Santa, and told him all the books were ready and all the games as well. The elves soon brought out great parcels of them, and they too were packed in the sledge.

'Thank you,' said Santa, taking up the reins. 'Now I'm going back to the mayor, to sleep at his house for the night.'

The next day Santa Claus drove off to the pink fairies to get the doll's houses, and he was very pleased indeed with them.

'We've hung up frilly curtains in all the windows,' said the little fairies, 'and we've put down carpets to match the wallpapers in every room, and we've made all the sheets and blankets for the beds and polished up everything we could.'

Santa Claus peeped into one or two doll's houses.

'They're quite perfect,' he said, 'and I am awfully pleased. Pack them at the back of my sledge please. There's room there.'

It took such a long time to pack them in properly that Santa had no time to do anything more that day, except drive straight to the mayor's.

He took three days seeing over the forts that the gnomes had made, and there were so many thousands of soldiers to look at that Santa Claus thought he would never come to the end.

'You've worked really splendidly,' he said to the busy little gnomes. 'Now put them in my sledge quickly. I've only one day left to collect the boxes of crackers from the red goblins, and then I must start on my travels for Christmas Eve.'

The next day he started off for the caves where the

red goblins lived. He left his sledge and reindeer outside the caves and strode into them. Not a single sound could he hear.

'Bless me! They're all asleep!' exclaimed Santa Claus in great astonishment.

Sure enough they were! They lay all around the middle cave, snoring.

'Wake up! Wake up! You lazy little creatures!' cried Santa, clapping his hands.

The red goblins sat up.

'Oh! Oh! Oh!' they cried. 'Here's Santa Claus, and we haven't finished our work!'

'Not finished your work!' thundered Santa Claus, frowning. 'What in the world do you mean!'

'Please, we didn't have enough gunpowder to put in the crackers, so we couldn't make enough!' explained a goblin, trembling.

'You *did* have enough; you had more than enough! I sent you the gunpowder myself!' roared Santa Claus. 'What have you done with it?'

'Please don't be so angry with us!' begged the goblins. 'You see we had a big party on November 5th, and we used some of the gunpowder to make fireworks with!'

'Then you're very, very naughty,' said Santa Claus, 'and I shall punish you. Put the crackers you have made into my sledge at once, and come to the mayor's house after Christmas, and I will tell you what your punishment is to be!'

The goblins scurried about and Santa Claus scolded them. They were very sulky and sullen and glared at him whenever he spoke.

At last he went outside to get into his sledge. But it wasn't there!

'Where are my reindeer?' shouted Santa Claus.

'He, he! Ha, ha! Ho, ho!' laughed the wicked red goblins. 'You were cross with us, and now our two chief goblins have driven your sledge away, and you won't have any toys for Christmas!'

Santa Claus was in a terrible state of mind. He

rushed into a shop nearby and bought a toy motorcar.

This will catch them up perhaps! he thought desperately. He wound up the motorcar, jumped in and started off. He saw the track of the reindeer on the road, and followed it as quickly as ever the toy motorcar could go.

On and on and on he went, swishing round corners, sounding his horn continuously.

Suddenly, far away in front of him, he heard the sound of sleigh bells.

'Hurray! I shall catch them before long!' yelled Santa. But just at that moment the toy motorcar stopped, and he had to get out and wind the clockwork up again. By that time he could hear the sleigh bells no more.

Presently it became dark, but still Santa Claus drove on and on and on, always listening for the tinkling sleigh bells.

All through the night he drove, until the day dawned.

'Goodness me! I'm right out of Toyland! I'm in the country of the North Wind!' exclaimed Santa as he looked around, and got out to wind up his motorcar again. 'And, oh! Thank goodness, there's my sledge not very far in front of me!'

Santa Claus drove furiously, and at last caught up to the sledge! He blew a silver whistle that he had hanging round his neck, and at once the reindeer stopped, in spite of the two red goblins who were whipping them to make them go on.

Santa got out of the motorcar, and at the same moment the North Wind came up to see what the disturbance was.

'I give you these two red goblins as your prisoners,' said Santa Claus sternly. 'They have driven off with my sledge of toys, and tomorrow is Christmas Day! I shall only just have time to get to the world of boys and girls by evening now.'

'I'll keep them safely!' said the North Wind, grabbing hold of the wicked goblins and shaking them.

'Gee up! Gee up!' called Santa Claus to his reindeer.

But, alas! They had no sooner gone forward a step or two than all the reindeer fell down, gasping.

'Oh, dear, dear, dear!' cried poor Santa Claus in despair. 'Whatever *shall* I do! I *must* get the toys to the children somehow!'

'Take them in the toy motorcar,' suggested the North Wind.

'It's *much* too small,' said Santa Claus sadly.

'Oh, I can soon alter *that*,' laughed the North Wind. 'And as you've given me two prisoners to keep as servants, I'll be very pleased to!'

He suddenly pursed up his mouth and blew towards the toy motorcar three times. Immediately it grew to a tremendous size.

'Goodness!' gasped Santa Claus. 'That's splendid! Now then, you two goblins, I'll give you just half an hour to unpack all the toys out of the sledge and pack them in the motorcar!'

The two frightened goblins set to work, and soon

all the toys were neatly packed into the car.

'Now I'm off!' said Santa Claus, getting into the car and taking hold of the steering wheel. 'Don't bother about my reindeer, they'll go back to their stables by themselves when they feel better. Goodbye!' And off drove Santa Claus as fast as ever the car would go!

And that Christmas night no child heard the sound of sleigh bells as Santa Claus went his rounds.

'But I heard the sound of a great motor,' said one little boy to his mother. 'And when I looked out of the window to see why, there was a great motorcar full of toys, and Santa Claus was driving it!'

'Nonsense!' said his mother, smiling. 'You must have dreamt it! Santa Claus never uses a motorcar!'

But he did that year, and if that Christmas Eve *you* were awakened by the sound of a motor in the middle of the night, you will know what it was – it was the toy motorcar Santa Claus had to use when the red goblins ran away with his reindeer!

The Grateful Pig

The Grateful Pig

PETER HAD a lovely collection of toys for Christmas. One of them was a balloon pig that he could blow up and stand on the table. He could put a small cork into the blow tube, and then the pig would stand for hours, as fat and big as could be. But when Peter took out the cork all the air in the pig rushed out, shrieking and wailing. It was very funny to see it getting smaller and smaller, howling as it grew little and then collapsing into a tiny heap of flat rubber.

The pig liked to be blown up. It hated to be flat. It couldn't see anything then, and it felt dull. It loved to be big and fat, and to stand up so that it could look round the nursery. What it wanted more than anything else was to stand on the mantelpiece. From there it could see all round the nursery – but Peter had the mantelpiece full of Christmas cards, so the pig had to stand on a low table, where it could see very little.

Before Peter went to bed he blew the pig up till it was really quite enormous and half afraid it would burst. But it didn't. Peter put the cork into the blow tube and stood the pig on the low table. 'There!' he said. 'You shall guard all my toys tonight, pig.'

The pig felt proud. It stood on the table on its four short legs till the night grew dark and very late. Everyone had gone to bed. There was no sound except the ticking of the dining-room clock. The sailor doll came to sit by the pig for company, and they began to talk – but suddenly they heard a low sound. The window was opening and someone was climbing in!

'A burglar!' whispered the sailor doll in a fright. The pig trembled and shook. Was it someone come to steal Peter's toys?

It *was* a burglar. He had come to see if he could find some jewellery to steal – but the balloon pig thought he had come to take the sailor doll, the teddy bear and the train. What could he do to stop that burglar? Peter had told him to guard his toys, and so he must.

An idea came into his little piggy head. He whispered to the sailor doll, 'Pull the cork out of my blow tube. Then I shall go flat and make a most terrible wailing, crying noise, which will frighten the burglar terribly.'

'But if you go flat you can't see anything, and you hate that,' said the sailor doll.

'Never mind,' said the pig, sighing. 'I must put up with that. Go on, pull out the cork.'

So the sailor doll pulled out the little cork and the balloon pig began to grow smaller and smaller. As he went flat he shrieked and wailed very loudly indeed, and the burglar was frightened out of his life! He stood as if he were frozen, and all his hair stood straight up. Whatever could that dreadful noise be near to him? He turned and fled to the window, jumped out, fell on his nose on the bed beneath, and then tore down the street as if a thousand dogs were after him.

Everyone woke up – and when they saw that it was the pig that had frightened the burglar away, how pleased they were! 'He shall be blown up again and live on the mantelpiece!' said Peter. So he got his wish, and there he is, as fat as a real pig and as happy as a sandboy, standing on his four short legs high up on the mantelpiece.

They Quite Forgot!

They Quite Forgot!

'DOESN'T GRANDPA give us lovely presents?' said Hilary, looking at the walking, talking doll she had been given for Christmas. 'This is my very best present of all!'

'Well, what about *my* present?' said Donald. 'I bet he spent even more money on that model yacht he sent me than on your doll. It's better than any yacht on the pond – you should see how the boys stare when I sail it there.'

'Last year Grandpa gave me my doll's house for Christmas, and when my birthday came in January he sent me all the furniture for it,' said Hilary, remembering. 'He sent *you* a railway train at Christmas and a station and signals for your birthday.'

Mother was listening. 'Yes, Grandpa's very kind to you, twins,' she said. 'But, you know, he was very upset last Christmas because you forgot to write and thank him for his present.'

'Oh, dear! Thank-you letters are a bore!' said Hilary. She looked at her twin. 'Aren't they, Donald?'

'Yes,' said Donald.

'They happen to be good manners,' said Mother.

'Good manners are a bigger bore!' said Donald.

'Really?' said Mother. 'I'm sorry it bores you to open the door for me, Donald, or to carry my basket or let me go first into a room.'

'It doesn't bore me to do those things, Mother,' said Donald, going red. 'You know it doesn't. Anyway, I've written three thank-you letters already, which is pretty good.'

'Have you written to Grandpa?' asked Mother. 'Don't write him a scrappy, untidy note.'

'I'll write him a long letter,' promised Donald. 'So will Hilary. We only put it off because thank-you letters to Grandpa have to be very good ones.'

The telephone bell rang and Mother went out of the room. Donald kicked the leg of the table he was sitting at. 'Blow! Why did I say that about good manners? Now Mother won't ask me to carry her basket or go on errands – and I *like* doing things for her!'

'Shall we write those thank-you letters to Grandpa now?' said Hilary. 'It *was* kind of him to send those smashing presents.'

'All right,' said Donald – but just as he was getting his fountain pen and some paper, he saw his friend Alec coming in at the gate.

'Oh, there's Alec – I forgot I had asked him to come round,' he said. 'Let's do the letters tonight, Hilary.'

Well, of course, they forgot. 'Blow, we didn't do them,' said Donald, as he got into bed. 'Never mind – Mother is sure to remind us!'

Mother didn't remind them. She didn't say another word about Grandpa, and the twins forgot all about the letters.

They remembered them two days before their birthday, which, of course, was on the same day. 'I say, we forgot to thank Grandpa for his Christmas presents!' said Hilary suddenly. 'How *awful* of us!'

'Gosh, so we did,' said Donald. 'Well, never mind – he'll be sending us our birthday presents in two days, and then we can write very, very nice thank-you letters for both the Christmas presents *and* the birthday presents.'

'Good idea!' said Hilary.

There were a lot of parcels on their birthday and dozens of cards. The twins looked hurriedly at their parcels.

'Let's leave Grandpa's presents till last,' they said. 'His are always the best.'

'They must be in this big parcel,' said Hilary. 'Mother, *look* at all the presents! Aren't we lucky?'

THEY QUITE FORGOT!

The twins opened their parcels – a book each from Auntie Meg. Notepaper with their initials on from Uncle Harry. A set of beautiful pencils each from Auntie Sue, and a dear little clock between them from their cousins – really, they did have some nice presents!

'Now for Grandpa's!' said Donald, and undid the big parcel in excitement. But it wasn't from Grandpa. It was from an old friend of their mother's, who had sent them a china cat and dog – and because they were breakable, had had them done up in tissue paper, cardboard and a box! No wonder the parcel looked enormous.

'There's nothing from Grandpa,' said Donald in surprise. 'Perhaps it will come by the next post.'

But nothing came by the second post except a few more cards and a book from a friend! How strange!

'Mother, Grandpa must have forgotten our birthday!' said Hilary, disappointed. 'He's never, never done that before!'

'Well, you can't possibly remind him,' said Mother.

The twins were sad. Grandpa's presents were always so grand.

'He *said* he wanted to give you a handbag, Hilary, and you an aeroplane, Donald,' said Mother. 'I distinctly remember him saying so just before Christmas.'

'Oh, blow!' said Hilary, almost in tears. 'A handbag! It would be a wizard one, I know – better than any the other girls have!'

Still, it was quite certain that Grandpa must have forgotten. He hadn't even sent them cards as he always did.

Then, that afternoon, Mother had a letter from Grandpa. The children knew the writing on the envelope and waited eagerly to see if there was a message for them.

'There isn't a message for you,' said Mother, looking up. 'But, oh, dear – listen to what Grandpa has written: *As the twins did not write to thank me for their Christmas presents I suppose they did not like them. I shall not bother to send them birthday presents, as I do not expect they would like those either.* Oh, *twins* – so you didn't keep your promise and write to thank Grandpa?'

The twins were both very red. 'No. We forgot after all,' said Donald. 'I'm sorry, Mother. Please don't look like that. I truly am sorry.'

'It's too late to be sorry now,' said Mother. 'I'm afraid you have hurt Grandpa and made him cross – such a *kind* old man too! He's ill in bed and doesn't sound very happy.'

'You'll make me cry on my birthday, Mother!' said Hilary, blinking tears away. 'And that's unlucky.'

Somehow the birthday was spoilt. After tea the twins looked at their presents again and then looked at each other.

'Hilary,' said Donald, 'I'm going to write to Grandpa straight away, and own up, and tell him I'm sorry. And I'm going to spend half my birthday money on some flowers for him because he's ill.'

'Oh, *what* a good idea!' said Hilary, cheering up. 'I'll do the same – but I'll spend my money on pears for him. He loves pears.'

Mother came into the room when they were writing quite a long letter each. The twins showed her what they had written. She read their letters in silence. Then she smiled.

'You're nicer children than I thought!' she said. 'Grandpa *will* be pleased. But you won't get any birthday presents from him this year, you know – I certainly wouldn't let him give you any, even if he wanted to.'

'We don't expect them,' said Donald. 'Gosh, I'll never forget again – how *horrid* he must have thought us! Now, tomorrow I'm going out to order some flowers.'

Grandpa was very, very pleased! In fact, he said he felt much better when he read those two nice letters. He got out of bed and went to a cupboard. He pulled out a blue handbag with a gilt handle, and a box with an aeroplane in. He wrote on a piece of paper, put it with the two presents – and put them back in the cupboard again. What had he written? Oh, just a few words to remind him to do something at Easter. This is what he had scribbled on the paper:

For the twins – to be sent to them for Easter *without fail.*

Wasn't it nice of him?

Mr Wittle's Snowball

Mr Wittle's Snowball

ONE COLD winter's day Mr Wittle put on his pixie hat, his thick coat and his spotted scarf and went out for a walk. He hadn't gone very far before it began to snow. Mr Wittle was delighted, for he had come from a warm land and had never in his life seen snow before.

This is beautiful stuff, he thought. *I will take some home with me and keep it.* So he gathered some snow in his hands and pressed it into a round ball. It was very cold indeed, but Mr Wittle liked the feel of it. He took the snowball home and put it down on the hearth. Then he took off his coat and hat and scarf, sat down and toasted his cold toes by the kitchen fire. And he fell *fast* asleep!

When he woke up the snowball had gone! He jumped up in a rage and shouted out, 'Who's stolen my snowball? Who's stolen my snowball?' Then off he ran to find out. A great many wood folk lived near him, and he was quite sure it was one of them that had stolen his precious snowball.

First he went to Little-Snout the hedgehog, and he found him curled up in a hole on the bank of the ditch, fast asleep. 'Wake up, wake up!' roared Mr Wittle. 'What have you done with my snowball? Have you eaten it?'

'No,' said Little-Snout crossly. 'I sleep all through the cold weather. Go away!'

Then Mr Wittle went to Slow-One the toad, who was hiding under a big stone not far away, his eyes tightly closed. 'Wake up, wake up!' shouted Mr Wittle. 'What have you done with my snowball, old coppery eyes?'

'Nothing,' said Slow-One sleepily. 'I don't know

what a snowball is. I'm asleep every day now.'

Then Mr Wittle went to the pond and called on Green-Back the frog. But he couldn't get any answer at all, for Green-Back and his brothers were sleeping soundly, standing on their heads in the mud at the bottom.

Then Mr Wittle went to Shelly the snail, but Shelly had made a hard little door at the bottom of his shell, and Mr Wittle couldn't make him open it. So he went off to Furry the dormouse, who was curled up in a heap of dry leaves in a hole in the ditch. 'Wake up, wake up!' shouted Mr Wittle. 'What have you done with my snowball?'

'Nothing,' said Furry, waking up with a jump. 'I don't know anything about snowballs. How should I? I sleep soundly all the winter through. And so would you, if you were sensible! Snowballs, indeed!' And he tucked his head away and fell asleep again.

Poor Mr Wittle! No one else lived near him, so there was nobody else to ask. He trudged home sadly, wondering and wondering who had stolen his precious white snowball.

Do *you* know who was the thief? Ah, perhaps his crackling kitchen fire could have told Mr Wittle who stole his snowball!

Look Out for the Snowman!

Look Out for the Snowman!

MOTHER TUPPENY was puzzled. She had twelve hens and, quite suddenly, they had almost stopped laying eggs for her.

'They have been laying so well,' she said to Mr Peeko next door. 'And now they hardly lay at all. What do you think is the matter with them? Shall I give them some medicine or scold them or what?'

'No, no,' said Mr Peeko. 'Your hens look healthy enough, Mother Tuppeny. Perhaps your children have been running in and out, taking the eggs?'

'Oh, no. They always bring them to me when they find any in the nests,' said Mother Tuppeny. 'It's a great loss, Mr Peeko – I use such a lot of eggs for the children, you know. I don't know what to give them for breakfast now.'

'Now you listen to me, Mother Tuppeny,' said Mr Peeko, thinking hard. 'I believe a thief may be coming in the night and stealing your eggs. You leave two eggs in one of the nests, and see if they are there the next morning.'

So Mother Tuppeny left two eggs in the nest and looked for them the next morning. They were gone! What a shame! She ran crying to Mr Peeko.

'Those two eggs have gone – and there are none at all in the boxes. It's a thief who comes, Mr Peeko. What shall I do?'

'You go to Mr Plod, the policeman, and tell him all about it,' said Mr Peeko. 'He'll know what to do!'

So Mother Tuppeny went to Mr Plod. He listened gravely, then took out his big black notebook. 'Now you listen carefully to me and do exactly as I tell you, Mother Tuppeny,' he said. 'You go home and tell your children to make a nice big snowman near your hen house, and to leave it there tonight. And if you see me come into your garden when the moon is up, don't you take any notice.'

So Mother Tuppeny told her children to go and make a fine snowman in her garden by the hen house, and they rushed out in delight.

Soon a great big snowman was built there, with a big round head, a long white body, stones for eyes and buttons, and a twig for his mouth. Mother Tuppeny gave the children one of her old hats and an old shawl to dress him in.

'It's a snow-woman now, not a snowman,' cried the children. 'Oh, look, Mother, isn't she lovely?'

'Yes, lovely,' said Mother Tuppeny, laughing at the funny sight of the old snow-woman with her hat and shawl on. 'Now come along in and have tea. It will soon be dark.'

They left the snow-woman in the garden and went in to tea. When it got dark Mother Tuppeny thought she heard footsteps in the garden and she guessed it was Mr Plod.

So it was. He went down to the hen house and found the snow-woman. He flashed his torch on her and smiled. What a queer-looking creature!

Mr Plod knocked the old snow-woman down so that there was nothing left of her. Then he stood himself in her place, with a white mackintosh over his uniform. He put the old hat on his head, and dragged the red shawl round him. Then he stood quite still.

When the children lifted the curtain and peered out into the moonlight before they went to bed, they laughed.

'Look! There's our old snow-woman out there all alone! How queer she looks!'

'She looks taller than when we built her,' said one of the boys.

'Oh, no! How could she be?' said the other children. 'Snowmen don't grow!'

But, of course, theirs *had* grown, because Mr Plod

was quite a bit taller than the snow-woman they had built. He stood there very patiently, waiting and waiting.

Nobody came for a long, long time. Then from over the wall at the bottom came a little knobbly figure.

Mr Plod tried to see who it was.

'Well, well, it's that nasty mean little Knobbly Goblin!' said Mr Plod to himself. 'I've often thought he was up to mischief – and so he is!'

The Knobbly Goblin crept to the hen house. He suddenly saw the snowman – or what he thought was a snowman – and he stopped in fright. Then he laughed a little goblin laugh.

'Ho, ho! You're only a snowman! You thought you could frighten me, standing there, watching. But you can't!'

He went into the hen house and came out with a bag full of eggs. Ha, ha! What a lovely lot!

He went up to the snowman. 'Silly old snowman! Wouldn't you like to tell tales of me? But you can't!'

And then, to the Knobbly Goblin's horror, an arm shot out from the snowman and a deep voice said, 'You just come along with me!'

He was held tightly in a big hand, and then he was shaken. 'Put down those eggs. You're a thief!' said the snowman.

The Knobbly Goblin was so frightened that he dropped the eggs. Luckily they fell into the snow and didn't break. 'P-p-p-please let me g-g-g-go,' he begged. 'Snowman, who are you? I've never met a live one before.'

Mr Plod didn't answer. He took the goblin to the police station – and there Knobbly saw that it was Mr Plod, the policeman, who had got him. Ooooooh!

Mr Plod went to see Mother Tuppeny the next day. 'I've scolded the thief,' he told her. 'It was that Knobbly Goblin. I've sent him away, and I've made him pay a fine of ten golden pieces to me. Here they are! They will help to pay for all the eggs he has stolen. I was that snowman, Mother Tuppeny!'

'Oh, how I wish I'd seen you all dressed up!' cried Mother Tuppeny. 'The children couldn't *think* what had happened to their snow-woman this morning. They were quite sad about her.'

'You buy them some sweets,' said Mr Plod. 'And tell them how I put on the hat and shawl. They won't mind a bit then!'

They didn't, of course. They laughed when they heard about it.

As for Knobbly, he simply can't bear the sight of a snowman now!

Santa Claus Goes to Mr Pink-Whistle

Santa Claus Goes to Mr Pink-Whistle

ONE CHRISTMAS night Santa Claus went out to set off as usual in his sleigh. As soon as he stepped out of the castle door, he stopped in dismay.

'What a wind!' he said as his red coat flapped round his legs. 'And my word, what snow! I'll be lucky if I find my way about tonight. Hey there, Trig and Trim – are the reindeer ready?'

Trig and Trim were the two little imps who went with Santa Claus in his sleigh. One of them drove the reindeer for him and the other helped him to tie and untie his sack of toys. They called back at once. 'Yes, Santa, they're ready, but they don't like this wind and snow! They are very restless indeed!'

Santa Claus got into the sleigh and settled down. 'I'd better drive,' he said, but, dear me, his hands were so cold that he soon had to hand the reins to Trig.

How the wind buffeted the sleigh as it sped through the sky that night! *Whoooo-oo!* it shouted, and almost deafened Santa Claus. Then there came such a snow squall that the reindeer couldn't see where they were going and galloped round in circles – and the sleigh almost turned on its side.

Out fell Trig and Trim with loud yells, and tumbled right down to earth, falling on banks of soft snow. Santa Claus had his eyes shut because of the snow and he didn't even see them go – so he was most surprised when he opened his eyes again and saw that he was the only one in the sleigh.

Good gracious! Now what am I to do? he thought, and he clutched at the loose reins to try to calm the reindeer. *I must get help. Things are certainly going very wrong tonight! But who can help me?*

And then he suddenly remembered dear old Mr Pink-Whistle, the little man who always puts wrong things right. *Perhaps he can do something for me*, thought Santa, pulling at the reins. 'Ho there, behave yourselves, reindeer – my sack of toys nearly fell out then. What would the children say if there were no toys in their stockings tomorrow morning?'

Santa Claus was a good way from where Mr Pink-Whistle lived, but the reindeer could go as fast as lightning if they chose – and very soon the sleigh was right over Pink-Whistle's little cottage. Sooty, his cat, suddenly heard the sound of sleigh bells and was astonished. 'Master!' he cried, running into Pink-Whistle's room. 'I can hear Santa coming!'

'Nonsense!' said Pink-Whistle, who was sitting cosily by the fire. 'There are no children here. You're mistaken.'

But just at that moment there came a thunderous knock at Pink-Whistle's door, and a great voice shouted loudly, 'Hey, Pink-Whistle – open the door, man. It's me, Santa Claus.'

Sooty and Pink-Whistle ran to the door together, astonished and delighted. Santa Claus came in, covered with snow, stamping his feet and rubbing his hands.

'Come in, come in! This is an honour!' said Pink-Whistle gladly. 'Sooty, fetch some hot drinks.'

'I can't stay, Pink-Whistle,' said Santa Claus. 'I've come for your help. You put things right when they go wrong, don't you?'

'I try to, sir, I always try to!' said Pink-Whistle, feeling even more surprised. 'But surely you don't want my help!'

'I do, I most certainly do!' said Santa Claus. 'My reindeer lost their way in this blizzard and ran round in circles, so that the sleigh almost tipped over – and Trig and Trim, my two helpers, fell out.'

'Good gracious!' said Pink-Whistle. 'Are they hurt?'

'Oh, no – they'll be all right,' said Santa Claus. 'There was thick snow on the ground; it'll feel like falling on a nice, soft feather bed, but I can't get them back, and I need help. You see, I have to keep looking at my notebook to see the names and addresses of children I am going to leave presents for, so someone must drive the reindeer – and I also need someone to tie and untie the sack for me, and hold it so that I can take out the toys I want.'

'I see,' said Pink-Whistle, frowning as he thought very hard indeed. 'Yes, you certainly must have help. Ah, here is Sooty with some hot drinks. What will you have, Santa – cocoa, tea, or hot lemon?'

'Well, I wouldn't mind some of all three,' said Santa. 'I'm so very cold. Feel my hands! How could I drive reindeer with hands as cold as that? Why, I couldn't even feel the reins!'

They sat sipping the hot drinks, and Pink-Whistle began to worry about how he could put things right for such an important person as Santa Claus. Sooty stood nearby and thought hard too.

'Well, can you think of a way to help me?' asked

Santa Claus, finishing his second cup of cocoa and starting on the tea. 'Don't you disappoint me now – I've heard great things of you, Pink-Whistle, yes, great things!'

'I can't think of anyone who would be able to drive reindeer through the sky,' said Pink-Whistle. 'I know a young air pilot who flies planes – but reindeer are different.'

'My dear fellow, of course they're different, but they're well trained,' said Santa. 'They're as easy to drive as horses, but they go much faster. Anyone who can drive horses would do – anyone!'

'There's nobody living near here that can drive,' said Pink-Whistle, beginning to feel quite desperate. 'And we'd never be able to get through this blizzard to the man who keeps the riding stables in the next village. Sooty, do you know anyone nearby who would be able to drive Santa's reindeer?'

'Oh, yes, master!' said Sooty, at once.

'Dear me – who?' said Pink-Whistle in surprise.

'Why, you!' said Sooty. 'And even if you couldn't drive, I'm sure it would be easy to manage well-trained reindeer.'

'Good gracious, yes, I suppose I could drive the sleigh!' said Pink-Whistle, suddenly excited. 'Where's my thick coat, Sooty? And I shall want a woolly scarf to tie my hat on my head. And I'll keep on my warm slippers or my feet will get cold. Dear me – what an idea!'

'A very, very good one!' said Santa Claus, beaming. 'It would be nice to have your company in the sleigh tonight, Pink-Whistle. You're a good fellow. I like you, and I'm not surprised that the children think of you as a friend! Right, you shall drive. But now – who can come and handle the big sack for me? What about your next-door neighbour?'

'They're away,' said Pink-Whistle. But again Sooty knew what to do.

'I'm coming!' he said, and his green eyes shone brightly. 'I can help with the sack. I'm used to helping

Mr Pink-Whistle in all kinds of ways, Santa Claus, and I know I can help you too. Please do let me come!'

'Well, what an idea!' said Pink-Whistle again. 'Yes, I don't see why you shouldn't come, Sooty. You're very clever and always helpful. Santa Claus, I think he'll manage the sack very well for you.'

'Splendid!' said the jolly old fellow, drinking the hot lemon juice. 'Well, can we start now? I feel much warmer. Even my hands are beginning to warm up. Feel them!'

Pink-Whistle was soon dressed warmly in his thickest topcoat, and had his hat tied firmly on his head with a woolly scarf. He kept his comfortable slippers on, and put his woollen gloves down to the fire to warm.

'You'd better borrow one of my short coats, Sooty,' said Pink-Whistle.

'Oh, no – I'll be quite warm enough in my own black fur coat!' said Sooty. 'I'll borrow one of your scarfs though, master. Are we ready now? The reindeer must be getting impatient, because I can hear their bells ringing very loudly.' Sooty put some coal on the fire, put the guard round it, turned out the lights and off they went out of doors into the snow.

'Thank goodness the wind isn't quite so fierce now,' said Santa Claus, looking around for his reindeer. 'Goodness me – is that mound over there my sleigh and reindeer? Why, they're covered with snow!'

So they were – and it was quite a job to get the snow off and climb into the sleigh. Pink-Whistle took the reins very proudly indeed, and the reindeer tossed their beautiful antlers and made their bells ring out loudly.

'You're not nervous, are you, Pink-Whistle?' asked Santa Claus.

'Not a bit,' said Pink-Whistle. 'This is one of the nicest jobs I've ever had to do to help anyone! Ready? Sooty, sit down, or you'll be blown out.'

They set off and in half a minute were galloping through the wind-blown sky. The snow had almost stopped falling now, so it was much easier to see the way. The reindeer knew it well, for they had galloped the same way for hundreds of years.

Pink-Whistle enjoyed himself very much indeed. So did Sooty – in fact, Sooty felt very important whenever he had to open the sack for Santa, and then tie it up safely again. Santa always knew exactly what to take out of it.

'See, I have a long list,' he said to Sooty, and showed it to him. 'I've written down on it all the things the children have asked me for. This boy John now, that we've just taken an aeroplane for out of the sack – here's his name – and see, I've written *Aeroplane* down beside it. I'd never remember all these things without my list. Thank goodness it didn't blow away in the wind! Now, I'll just climb down this chimney if you'll hold the reindeer still on the roof, Pink-Whistle. I've trained them not to stamp about on roofs, so they'll be quite quiet.'

It was really a very exciting night for Mr

Pink-Whistle and Sooty. They had never enjoyed themselves so much in all their lives. Sooty thought the sack of toys was marvellous – it always seemed as full as ever, no matter how many toys Santa took out of it.

'One child has asked for a clockwork mouse,' said Santa to Sooty. 'Aha! That's the kind of toy you'd like, wouldn't you? Now, just let me look at my list again. We're getting on!'

When all the toys had been put into the stockings of many, many children, Pink-Whistle drove back to his own little house again, and got out of the sleigh very regretfully. Sooty jumped out too, and ran indoors to fetch lumps of sugar for the reindeer.

'Can you drive yourself back home now, Santa?' asked Pink-Whistle. 'Let me feel your hands. Yes, they are lovely and warm.'

'Oh, I'll be all right now,' said Santa. 'The wind has dropped and it's much warmer – and I shan't have to delve into my sack any more. I shall just sit back in my seat and hold the reins loosely and let the reindeer gallop back home at top speed.'

'I have enjoyed going out with you on Christmas Eve and driving your reindeer,' said Pink-Whistle.

'Well, I'll know where to come to next time things go wrong,' said Santa Claus, shaking the reins and clicking to the reindeer, who were now all munching Sooty's lumps of sugar. 'Many, many thanks. Goodbye, Pink-Whistle, goodbye, Sooty!' And with a ringing of bells they were off!

Pink-Whistle and Sooty couldn't help feeling sad that their grand adventure was over. They went indoors together – and, will you believe it, there, on the table, was a present for each of them!

'A new top hat for me – and a great big clockwork mouse for you, Sooty!' said Pink-Whistle in surprise. 'How did Santa put them here without us knowing? Well, isn't he a grand old fellow!'

Yes, Mr Pink-Whistle, he is – and so are you!

The Boy Who
Was Left Out

The Boy Who Was Left Out

JOHN'S MOTHER was ill at Christmas time, so his daddy sent him to his granny's for a few days. John was unhappy, because, although he loved his granny, it was horrid not being at home for Christmas – and, besides, he would miss going to his cousin's party, and to his friend Harry's party too.

Granny gave him as nice a Christmas as she could. After Christmas, when John was looking out of the window one morning, he saw a cart going by carrying a most enormous Christmas tree. 'Look, Granny!' he cried. 'What is that big Christmas tree for?'

'That's for the children's party at the village hall,'

said Granny. 'Mrs Jolly always gives a party to all the village children after Christmas, and they have a fine Christmas tree.'

'Shall I be asked too?' said John, eagerly.

'No, you haven't been asked,' said Granny. 'You aren't really one of the village children, you see, and, besides, Mrs Jolly doesn't even know you are here with me!'

Poor John! He was to be left out of Mrs Jolly's party too, as well as out of the parties he really had been asked to. *It was a shame*, John thought. He wondered what sort of toys Mrs Jolly would put on the tree – how lovely it would look, all lit with candles and dressed with bright ornaments and toys!

Now two days later John went for a walk, and as he went along the bumpy little lane a motorcar passed him going to the village hall, laden with good things for the party next day, and with a great parcel of toys tied on to the back of the car for the Christmas tree. And do you know what happened just as the car passed

John? It went over a big hole in the lane, and the parcel of toys burst open! Seven or eight of them fell into the road – a train, a book, a spinning top, a doll and two or three more. The car went on – and there were the toys left in the road!

John stared at them. What did he do? What would *you* do?

'Look at that!' said John. 'A whole heap of toys – and no one in sight! I've been left out of all my parties – I don't see why I shouldn't pick up these toys and have them for myself. I can hide them away from Granny.'

He picked them up – but on the way home he began to think hard. *It's a horrid thing to do. It isn't honest. These toys are meant for the other children, and they will have to go without. It's nobody's fault that I am left out of the village party. I shall take the toys to the hall and give them to the people there who are decorating the tree. I shall think a lot better of myself if I do that!*

So off trudged John to the hall, and whom should

he see there but Mrs Jolly!

'Your car dropped these toys,' said John.

Mrs Jolly beamed at him. 'Good boy!' she said. 'Thank you. I shall see you at the party tomorrow, shan't I?'

'No,' said John. 'I haven't been asked. I'm just staying with my granny. I'm not really one of the village children!'

'What does that matter?' cried Mrs Jolly. 'We can't leave out a nice honest little boy like you! Come along tomorrow at three!'

So John's going, and I shouldn't be surprised if he has one of the very best presents off the tree! He will certainly have a good time, for there are balloons, sweets, oranges and crackers by the hundred – but John deserves a jolly good party, don't you think so?

The Little Christmas Tree

The Little Christmas Tree

THERE WAS once a little fir tree that hated Christmas time. When it saw the snow coming it shivered and shook from top to toe.

'What's the matter?' asked a rabbit who had come out to nibble at the bark of a big tree nearby.

'It's Christmas,' said the fir tree. 'It may mean nothing to you, rabbit, but it frightens me. You see, I'm big enough now to be a real proper Christmas tree at a party. I shall be pulled up by my roots and hung up in a shop. I shall be bought and carried home. I shall have sharp spikes stuck into my tender branches when I am decorated, and, worse than that, candles will be lit all over me. I shall be burnt, I know I shall!'

'Well, you're a funny sort of tree,' said the rabbit in surprise. 'Most fir trees are very proud to amuse the children.'

Just then a man came by with a spade. When he saw the little fir tree he dug it up and put it into a cart. Then he carried it away to the nearest town. It trembled all the way, for it knew that its time had come. Soon it was hung outside a shop, and presently a little girl came to buy it.

'Now I shall have sharp spikes set into my branches,' groaned the tree, 'and candles will burn me.'

The little girl carried the tree home and planted it in a round bed in the garden. The fir tree was so surprised, for it had thought it would be put into a tub. *I shan't be a Christmas tree after all!* it thought.

But it was. The little girl decorated it the next day and hung all kinds of presents on it – but what funny presents they were! The tree couldn't understand them at all. There were twelve bits of coconut, eight biscuits, ten crusts of bread, two strings of monkey nuts twisted round and round its branches, six pieces of suet and five sprays of millet seed hung all around it!

'Well, whatever is all this for?' wondered the tree in astonishment.

He soon knew on Christmas morning, for there came such a rustle and flutter of wings, such a twitter and chirping! Down flew all the birds in the garden and perched in the branches of the little fir tree. Robins and sparrows, thrushes and blackbirds, starlings and tits, finches and hedge sparrows, they all came and pecked eagerly at the presents on his branches.

'You're a birds' Christmas tree!' cried a big thrush to the little tree. 'You're put out here for us! And every Christmas you'll be decorated like this, and in between times you'll grow bigger and bigger in the garden! Aren't you happy?'

'I should think I am!' cried the fir tree, and you should have heard his branches rustle from top to toe!

The Christmas Present

The Christmas Present

'WHAT SHALL we give Mummy for Christmas, Jinny?' said Johnny.

'I've seen something I *know* she would like,' said Jinny. 'It's in the jeweller's shop window. Come and see, Johnny.'

So Johnny went down to the village with Jinny, and she showed him what she had seen. It was a small brooch, and in the middle of it was the letter M in blue.

'There, M for Mummy,' said Jinny. 'Wouldn't you love to see Mummy wearing a brooch like that, that *we* gave her?'

'Yes. It would be nice,' said Johnny. 'I'm sure Mummy would love it too. Then when people say to her, "Dear me, I didn't know your name was Margaret or Mollie or Mary," she can say, "It isn't! It's Mummy!"'

'It's five shillings,' said Jinny. 'That's a lot of money – especially as we have to buy presents for other people too.'

'We'd better try and earn some,' said Johnny. 'We'll ask Cook if she knows of a way we can earn money. We might chop wood or something.'

But Cook said nobody would let them chop wood. They would only chop their fingers instead. 'Now, I'll tell you what to do!' she said. 'You go down to old Mrs Kennet. She wants someone to do her shopping for her each day. She can't walk up and down the hill where she lives on these frosty, slippery mornings. I am sure she would give you a penny each errand.'

Well, Mrs Kennet was very pleased to see the twins,

and delighted to think they would fetch her shopping for her.

'I can take my doll's pram to fetch it in,' said Jinny. 'And Johnny can take his barrow. Then we can bring quite a lot back for you, Mrs Kennet – potatoes and cabbages and all kinds of things. It will be fun.'

'It will be a good job of work,' said the old lady. 'Good work never hurt anyone – and good work should be paid for. I'm sure you are saving up to buy Christmas presents, aren't you? Well, I will pay you each tuppence every time you fetch my goods for me – that will be fourpence between you!'

'That won't be too much for you to pay, will it?' asked Jinny. 'We really meant to do it for only a penny a time.'

'Well, I'm paying you tuppence because of your having to come up this steep hill,' said Mrs Kennet. 'That's only fair. Now, you can begin today, if you like. The greengrocer has some carrots and onions for me, I want a loaf of brown bread, and a book from the library and a bag of flour.'

It was quite a lot of shopping to do. Jinny took her empty pram and Johnny took his little barrow. They got all the things that Mrs Kennet wanted, and then wheeled them up the hill to her house.

She was pleased. 'Here is your fourpence,' she said, and she gave two brown pennies to Jinny and two to Johnny. They ran home in glee and put them into their moneyboxes.

They told Mummy what they were doing for Mrs Kennet. Mummy said she thought they ought to help the old lady for nothing, but still, as they were saving up for Christmas, she was sure that Mrs Kennet was pleased to pay them.

'But you must do *some* of her errands for nothing,' said Mummy. 'Just to show her that you can be kind for no payment at all.'

So every third time they went on errands for Mrs Kennet the twins wouldn't take the pennies. 'We're doing your shopping today for nothing,' they told her. 'We want to.'

Each day they counted up their money for Mummy's Christmas present. And on the day before Christmas, what a wonderful thing – they had earned five shillings and fourpence between them!

'*Now* we can go and buy the brooch with M on,' said Jinny, and off they went.

They pushed open the door of the little jeweller's shop and went inside.

'Please can we have the brooch with M on?' asked Johnny, putting five shillings down on the counter. 'We want it for our mother.'

'Oh, dear – we sold it yesterday!' said the girl. 'I'm so sorry. It was the only one we had!'

The twins were dreadfully disappointed. They looked around the shop, trying to find something else that Mummy might like – but everything was so very, very dear. They hadn't nearly enough money!

They went out. Jinny's eyes were full of tears. 'Tomorrow's Christmas Day,' she said. 'And most of the shops have sold their nice things. We shan't be able to choose anything nice for Mummy now.'

Johnny had his little barrow with him, because Mrs Kennet had asked him to bring back her turkey from the butcher's. 'We'd better take this turkey to Mrs Kennet,' he said. 'She said she was waiting for it. We might have time to run down to the village afterwards and find something for Mummy.'

They took the turkey in the barrow all the way up the hill. Mrs Kennet asked them in. 'I've got some chocolate buns for you,' she said. 'Dear me, what solemn faces! Whatever is the matter?'

'Oh, Mrs Kennet!' said Jinny. 'We've been working for you all this time, and saving up to buy Mummy a lovely brooch – and now it's sold. And it's too late to buy Mummy anything nice now. All the best things are gone.'

'Well, that's very sad,' said Mrs Kennet. 'But wait a minute – let me see now – I've some jewellery I am going to sell. Maybe I have a little brooch that your mother would like – one that I could give you, because you've been so very, very good to me.'

'That wouldn't do,' said Johnny. 'We've earned the money and we wanted to *spend* it on Mummy. It wouldn't be the same if you just gave it to us for her. It wouldn't really be from us then.'

'Well, then, you may buy it from me, if you feel like that,' said Mrs Kennet, smiling. 'I'll fetch my jewellery case.'

She came back with a big leather box. She undid it – and, oh, what a lot of pretty things were there! Brooches, bracelets, necklaces, pins – but most of them were old and had lost their glitter and shine – and some were broken.

Suddenly Jinny gave a cry and pounced on a little brooch. 'Look! LOOK! Here's a brooch with M on it – and tiny little blue forget-me-nots all round it. It's much, much prettier than the one in the shop. Oh, Mrs Kennet, did one of your children give this to you years ago?'

'No,' said Mrs Kennet. 'It belonged to my aunt. Her name was Mary-Ann – and that's why the brooch has M on it. M for Mary-Ann. I was going to sell it – but if you like it, well, I will sell it to *you*! The letter M on it will do quite well for Mummy.'

'Is it very expensive?' asked Jinny. 'It's so very pretty, I'm afraid it will cost more money than we've got.'

'It's five shillings,' said Mrs Kennet, and the twins gave a shout of joy.

'We've got more than that! Can we clean the brooch and take it home with us? Here's the money, Mrs Kennet. Oh, it's a much, much nicer brooch than the other one!'

They cleaned the brooch, put it into a little box and took it home. They wrote a loving little message and put it on the breakfast table for Mummy the next morning.

'Oh!' she said, when she opened it. 'Twins! What a wonderful present! M for Mummy – and forget-me-nots all round it. Oh, it's my *nicest* present!'

'Yes, M for Mummy – and forget-me-nots to tell you we'll never, never forget you!' said Johnny, giving Mummy a hug. 'I'm *glad* you like it.'

Mummy did. She wears the brooch every single day. Wasn't it a wonderful Christmas present?

One Christmas Eve

One Christmas Eve

ONCE UPON a time there was a little boy who thought that Santa Claus must be the kindest, jolliest person in all the world.

When John remembered all the thousands of stockings Santa Claus had filled, all the thousands of sooty chimneys he had climbed down, and the many times he had gone back to his castle, cold and tired out late on Christmas Eve, he wondered and wondered if there was anyone to welcome Santa back – whether his slippers had been put to warm, and if anyone waited up at the castle to ask him how he had got on.

Now John lived not far from the hill on which

Santa Claus had his castle – so the little boy was lucky enough to see him sometimes, and say good morning very shyly. As Christmas came near one year, a plan came into John's mind – Santa was always giving other people surprises, it was quite time he had one himself!

So on Christmas Eve, after he had been put to bed, John got up again and dressed himself. He slipped out of doors and ran to the hill where Santa's castle stood, gleaming in the moonlight. In his hand he carried a big parcel. When he came to the castle he saw that the door was open, and he knew that Santa Claus had left with his reindeer to fill all the stockings.

John slipped into the castle. He went upstairs and found Santa's bedroom. It was cold and draughty. The little boy shut the windows, and put a match to the fire. Soon it was roaring up the chimney. John piled logs on to it, and then he looked round for Santa Claus's slippers. He put them on the fender to warm, found a kettle and put it on to boil, and placed on a little table a tin of cocoa he had brought and some milk.

Then quickly he found a large stocking, and hung it at the end of the bed. Into it he put a large-sized pipe, a packet of tobacco, an enormous white handkerchief and a very large pair of woolly gloves that he had asked his mother to knit for him. Then out he crept again, smiling all over his kind little face.

Now that night Santa Claus had had a very hard time. One of his reindeer had gone lame, so he couldn't go as quickly as he wanted to. He had stuck fast in two chimneys, and made himself very sooty before he had managed to get out. He had dropped one of his gloves somewhere, so that his right hand was as cold as ice and ached badly. In fact, altogether he was feeling rather miserable – and then, dear me, he couldn't get a large rocking horse down a chimney, and he had to go and knock at the door and give it to the surprised mother – a thing he always hated to do.

When he got home to his castle he was grumbling

away to himself. 'What's the sense of doing this every year? I'm an old man now – why should I bother to go out like this on a winter's night, taking a heavy sack of toys with me for children who never even think of writing a thank-you letter, lots of them? It's the last time I'll do it – the very last time!'

And then he saw his beautiful big fire – and his warm slippers – and the cocoa standing ready to be made – and his lovely fat stocking full of just the things he wanted!

'Some child has been here!' he said. 'Would you believe it! Well, well, well, to think how I've been grumbling tonight! I'm ashamed of myself, really I am! I shall never stop being Santa Claus, never, so long as there are children in the world. Just look what one has done for me, the generous little soul!'

And, my dears, ever since then Santa Claus has been about as usual at Christmas time. *Wasn't* it lucky that John gave him a surprise that Christmas Eve?

The Strange
Christmas Tree

The Strange Christmas Tree

ONCE UPON a time there was a Christmas tree that had been planted by a pixie. But before the tree had grown more than an inch or two high the pixie had gone away – so the tree grew in the wood all by itself, and didn't even know that it was a Christmas tree, for it had never been used at Christmas time at all.

But one Christmas a woodman came by and saw the tree, which had now grown into a fine big one. The man stopped and took his spade from his shoulder.

I could dig that tree up and sell it for a Christmas tree, he thought. *It would fetch a few pounds at least! I'll take it to market tomorrow.*

So he dug it up, put it into a great pot, and staggered to market with it.

And to the market came a mother and her three children. They saw the tree, and the children shouted in delight.

'Mother! Buy this tree! It's the biggest and the best one here.'

So the mother bought the tree, and the woodman carried it home for her.

The tree was astonished. What in the world was happening to it? It knew the fairy folk very well indeed, for it had lived with them for years, and knew their gentle ways and little high voices. But this world was something quite different – the people were big and tall, not like the fairy folk – and, how strange, they took trees into their houses and stood them there!

The Christmas tree didn't know about Christmas time. It stood in a corner of a big room in its pot, wondering what would happen next.

The children's mother came in with boxes of toys and ornaments and candles. Soon she had hung dozens of them on the tree, and it began to sparkle and shine as if it were a magic thing. It caught sight of itself in the mirror, and how astonished it was!

'I am beautiful!' said the tree. 'I glitter and shine. I am hung with the most beautiful things! Oh, I like living in this land, and being dressed up like this. I shall have a lovely time here!'

Now the children's mother had told them they must not even peep into the room where she had put the lovely Christmas tree. But, alas! They were disobedient children, and they meant to see the tree as soon as their mother had gone out.

So that night they all three slipped into the room to see the tree.

'It looks nice,' said Doris.

'It's not so big as the one last year,' said George.

'It hasn't got enough toys on,' said Kenneth.

'There's something *I* mean to get anyway!' said

Doris, pointing to a box of crackers. 'So don't you ask for that, boys!'

'Don't be mean, Doris,' said George. 'You got the crackers last year. It's my turn!'

'Well, I'm going to have the soldiers,' said Kenneth, and he took hold of a box of them. 'There's only one box this year, George, and as I'm the oldest I'm going to have them. See?'

'Don't be so mean and horrid!' said George.

'Look! Look!' said Doris suddenly. 'Here's a box of chocolates. Shall we undo the lid and take some? Nobody will know.'

Now wasn't that a horrid, mean thing to do? Children who do things like that don't deserve a lovely Christmas tree, and that's just what the tree thought. But it stood there quite still and silent, listening and looking.

The children took the chocolates – but Doris had the biggest one, so they began to quarrel again. George shoved Doris, and then Doris pushed Kenneth, and soon they were all fighting. The tree had never seen such behaviour before.

The children bumped against the tree and knocked off a lovely pink glass ornament. It fell to the floor and broke.

'Silly tree!' said Doris rudely. 'Why can't you hold things properly? Why aren't you as big as last year's tree? You're not half so pretty!'

'Christmas trees are babyish things,' said Kenneth. 'I vote we ask for a bran tub next year.'

'Yes, who wants a silly old tree now?' said George. 'We're getting too big.'

Then a noise was heard in the hall outside and the children fled, for it was their mother coming home. The tree was left alone, sad and angry. What dreadful children! How it hated staying in their house! But where could it go? It did not know its way back to the wood.

And then the tree saw four little faces pressed against the window, looking in, and heard whispering voices. It was the children of the poor woman down the lane. They had never had a Christmas tree in their lives, and nobody ever gave them Christmas presents, not even their mother, who was far too poor to give them even an orange each.

So the children had come to look at the Christmas tree in the big house.

'It's the most beautiful thing in the world!' said Ida.

'If only I could see all its candles alight and shining, I would always be happy when I remembered it,' said Lucy.

'Wouldn't Mother love that box of chocolates?' said Harry.

'I wouldn't want any of those toys for myself,' said Fred. 'I'd just be happy cutting them off the tree and giving them to Mother and to you others.'

The tree listened in surprise and delight. What different children these were. If only it was in *their* home.

Then there came the noise of an opening door and

the tree heard George's angry voice. 'There are some children peeping in our windows at our Christmas tree. Go away, you bad, naughty children. You're not to look at our tree!'

The four children ran off at once, afraid.

The tree felt angrier than ever. It shivered from top to toe at the thought of that horrid, unkind little boy! It stood there, wishing and wishing that it could leave the house.

And then suddenly it remembered some magic it had learnt from the fairy folk, and it murmured the words to itself. Its roots loosened in the pot. One big one put itself outside – and then another and another – and do you know, in a few moments, that strange Christmas tree was walking on its roots around the room! How strange it looked!

The door was open and the tree went out. The front door was shut, but the garden door was open for the cat to come in. The tree walked out of it just as the cat came in. The cat gave a scared mew and fled outside again. It wasn't used to trees walking out of a house!

The tree walked down the path and out of the gate. It saw the four children away in the distance, running to their home in the moonlight. Slowly and softly the Christmas tree followed them. But when it got to their house the door was shut!

The tree didn't mind at all. It preferred to wait in the garden, because its roots liked the feel of the earth.

There was no front garden but there was a small one at the back. So the tree walked round and stood there in the middle. It squeezed its roots into the soil and held itself there firmly, a marvellous sight with all its beautiful toys and ornaments and candles.

Then it called to the fairy folk, and they came in wonder. 'Light my candles for me,' rustled the tree, 'and then knock on the children's window.'

So the little folk lit all the candles and then rapped loudly on the children's window. Harry pulled back the curtain – and there was the tree standing in the little back garden, lit from top to toe, shining softly and beautifully, sparkling and glittering in a wonderful way.

'Look!' shouted Harry. 'Look!' And all the other children crowded to the window, with their mother behind them.

'A Christmas tree for us in our own garden!' shouted Lucy. 'Oh, it's like the one we saw in the big house.'

Harry ran out and shouted to the others in surprise. 'It's *growing* in the ground – it's really growing! It must be magic!'

Everyone crowded round it. The tree was very happy and glowed brightly. The children gently touched the toys. Harry cut off the box of chocolates and gave it to his mother.

And then Fred cut off the toys and pressed them into everybody's hands. He didn't want any for himself – he was so pleased to be able to give them to those he loved! But Harry made him have the box of soldiers and the red train.

Then they all went indoors out of the cold and left the Christmas tree by itself, still with its candles burning brightly. And that night the fairy folk took it back to its old place in the wood, where it grows to this day, remembering every Christmas time how once it wore candles and ornaments and toys.

As for Doris and George and Kenneth, what do you suppose they thought when they went to have their Christmas tree and found it was gone? Only the big pot was left, and nothing else at all! How they cried! How they sobbed! But I can't help being glad that the tree walked off to the children down the lane!

The Cold Snowman

The Cold Snowman

IT HAPPENED once that some children built a great big snowman. You should have seen him! He was as tall as you, but much fatter, and he wore an old top hat, so he looked very grand. On his hands were woollen gloves, but they were rather holey. Down his front were large round pebbles for buttons and round his neck was an old woollen scarf. He really looked very grand indeed.

The children went indoors at teatime, and didn't come out again because it was dark. So the snowman stood all alone in the backyard, and he was very lonely.

He began to sigh, and Foolish-One, the little elf who lived under the old apple tree, heard him and felt sorry. He ran out and spoke to the snowman.

'Are you lonely?' he asked.

'Very,' answered the snowman.

'Are you cold?' asked Foolish-One.

'Who wouldn't be in this frosty weather?' said the snowman.

'I'm sorry for you,' said Foolish-One. 'Shall I sing to you?'

'If you like,' said the snowman. So the elf began to sing a doleful little song about a star that fell from the sky and couldn't get back. It was so sad that the snowman cried a few tears, and they froze at once on his white, snowy cheeks.

'Stop singing that song,' he begged the elf. 'It makes me cry, and it is very painful to do that when your tears freeze on you. Oooh! Isn't the wind cold?'

'Poor snowman!' said Foolish-One, tying the snowman's scarf so tightly that he nearly choked.

'Don't do that!' gasped the snowman. 'You're strangling me.'

'You have no coat,' said Foolish-One, looking sadly at the snowman. 'You will be frozen stiff before morning.'

'Oooh!' said the snowman in alarm. 'Frozen stiff! That sounds dreadful! I wish I wasn't so cold.'

'Shall I get you a nice warm coat?' asked the elf. 'I have one that would keep you very cosy.'

'Well, seeing that you only come up to my knees, I'm afraid that your coat would only be big enough for a handkerchief for me,' said the snowman. 'Oooh! There's that cold wind again.'

Just then a smell of burning came over the air, and the elf sniffed it. He jumped to his feet in excitement. Just the thing!

'Snowman!' he cried. 'There's a bonfire. I can smell it. Let us go to it and warm ourselves.'

The snowman tried to move. He was very heavy, and little bits of snow broke off him. But at last he managed to shuffle along somehow, and he followed the dancing elf down the garden path to the corner of the garden where the bonfire was burning.

'Here we are!' said the elf in delight. 'See what a fine blaze there is. Come, snowman, draw close, and I will tell you a story.'

The snowman came as close to the fire as he could. It was certainly very warm. He couldn't feel the cold wind at all now. It was much better.

'Once upon a time,' began the elf, 'there was a princess called Marigold. Are you nice and warm, snowman?'

'Very,' said the snowman drowsily. The heat was making him sleepy. 'Go on, Foolish-One.'

'Now this princess lived in a high castle,' went on Foolish-One, leaning against the snowman as he talked. 'And one day – are you sure you're quite warm, snowman?'

'Very, very warm,' murmured the snowman, his hat slipping to one side of his head. Plonk! One of his stone buttons fell off. Plonk! Then another. How odd!

Foolish-One went on with his story. It wasn't a very exciting one, and the snowman hardly listened. He was so warm and sleepy. Foolish-One suddenly felt sleepy too. He stopped in the middle of his tale and shut his eyes. Then very gently he began to snore.

He woke up with a dreadful jump, for he heard a most peculiar noise.

Sizzle-sizzle-sizzle, *ss-ss-sss-ss*!

Whatever could it be? He jumped up. The fire was almost out. The snowman had gone! Only his hat, scarf and gloves remained, and they were in a pile on the ground.

'Who has put the fire out?' cried Foolish-One in a rage. 'Snowman, where are you? Why have you gone off and left all your clothes? You will catch your death of cold!'

But the snowman didn't answer. He was certainly quite gone. Foolish-One began to cry. The fire was quite out now, and a pool of water lay all round it. Who had poured the water there? And where, oh where, was that nice snowman?

He called him up the garden and down. He hunted for him everywhere. Then he went home and found his thickest coat and warmest hat. He put them on, took his stick and went out.

'I will find that snowman if it takes me a thousand years to do it!' he cried. And off he went to begin his search. He hasn't found him yet! Poor Foolish-One, I don't somehow think he ever will!

It's Like Magic!

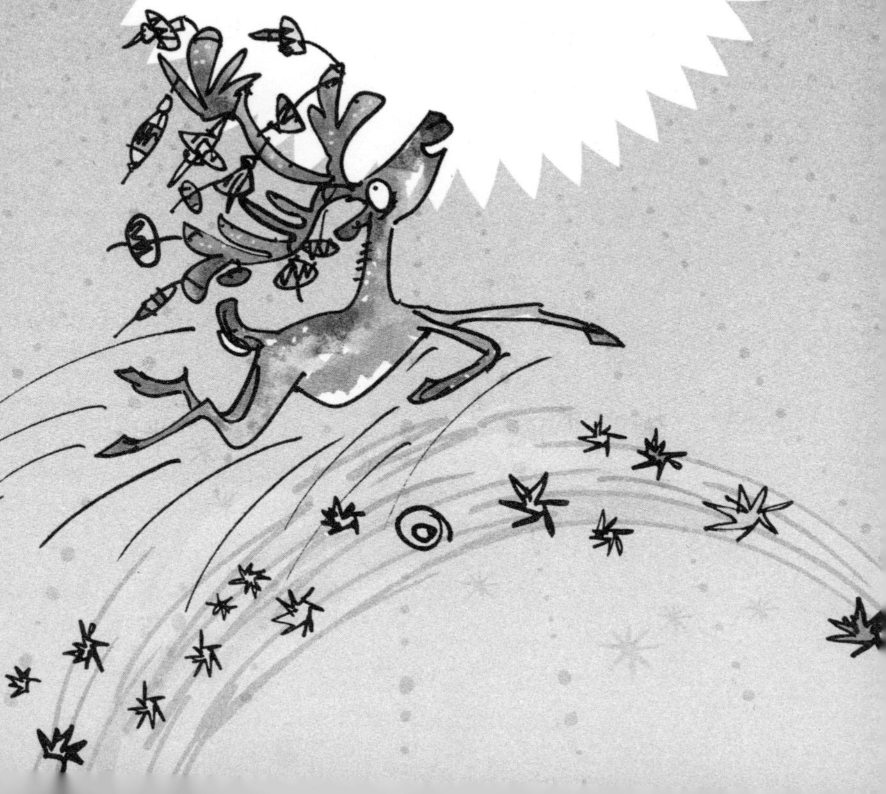

It's Like Magic!

DICK AND Susan were doing their homework one cold Saturday morning. It was snowing and they longed to go out, but Mother had said no, not till their homework was done.

Granny and Grandpa had called in, and were sitting chatting with Mother. Granny glanced over at the two children. 'I do hope we aren't making it difficult for them to do their homework,' she said. 'Talking away like this.'

'Oh, no, Granny,' said Dick. 'I'm drawing a map, so I can listen to all the exciting things you're saying – and Susan's making a pattern.'

'A pattern?' said Granny. 'What kind?'

'Oh, Granny – don't look at it!' said Susan, covering the page with her hand as Granny came over. 'In our drawing lessons at school we are learning to design patterns – but I simply *can't*.'

'Ha! Patterns!' said Grandpa, and he came over too. 'Now, *I* used to design patterns once – yes, for wallpaper! You didn't know that, did you? And some very pretty ones I designed too. You look at the wallpaper on Granny's bedroom wall next time you come – it's one of *my* designs!'

'Well, I never knew that before!' said Susan. 'Look, Grandpa, this is what we have to do – we can take a cross like + – or one like this, X – or a six-sided one like a little star, and make it a basis for a pattern repeated over the page. Well, how *can* I think of any good design to make out of a four-sided or six-sided cross?'

'I know someone who can make the most *miraculous* designs from a six-sided cross,' said Grandpa at once.

'And, do you know, although he has made thousands upon thousands of six-sided patterns, not one is the same! They are all different – and too beautiful for words!'

'Well, I wish I could make just *one*!' said Susan.

'Who's this pattern-maker you know?' asked Mummy, astonished.

'His name is Mr Frost,' said Grandpa solemnly. 'And I can show you some of his beautiful work this very minute if you like. You could even copy some of it for your homework, Susan.'

'We're not allowed to copy,' said Dick.

'Oh, this kind of copying would be allowed, I'm sure,' said Grandpa. 'Now, let me see – I want a nice bit of very black cloth – and has anyone a magnifying glass?'

The children stared at Grandpa in surprise. Black cloth – and a magnifying glass – what *was* he going to do?

'Here's a piece of black cloth,' said Mother, taking

a strip from her rag bag. 'And there's a magnifying glass in the desk over there. Get it, Susan.'

Susan fetched her father's magnifying glass. It was fun to look through it and see things magnified and made simply enormous. She had once looked at a small spider through it and what a surprise she got – it had looked extraordinary!

'And now we'll put on our coats and go out into the snow,' said Grandpa, 'because it is there we shall find some of the most beautiful designs in the whole world.'

Feeling really puzzled, the children put on their coats and went out with Grandpa. They felt the soft snowflakes falling all around them, touching them with cold little fingers. Now, where were these patterns that Grandpa kept talking about?

'Come close to me,' said Grandpa, 'and see me catch a snowflake or two on this piece of black cloth. Did you know that they are made of tiny glittering crystals? Now look – I've caught one – quick, take the magnifying glass, Susan, and look at it closely.'

Susan gazed through the magnifying glass and gasped. 'Grandpa! You're right – it *is* made of tiny brilliant crystals – how beautiful!'

'Count how many sides the crystal has that you are looking at,' said Grandpa.

'Six!' said Susan, counting. 'And so has the next one – and, oh, there's another snowflake on the black cloth now, all made of tiny crystals too, and, let me see – yes – every single one is six-sided!'

'Let *me* look,' said Dick, and he took the magnifying glass eagerly. 'Whew! How beautiful – and you're right, they *are* all six-sided. But, wait a minute, here's one that's got more sides – yes, twelve!'

'Well, that's *twice* six,' said Grandpa. 'And you may find one with three-times six sides – always the snow crystals will be six-sided, or a multiple of six. But do you notice that every single one is different? Each crystal with its six arms shows different designs, never one the same!'

'Look at this one – oh, I shall *have* to draw it when I get indoors!' cried Susan. 'See, the one that looks like a six-sided leaf – and this one that's rather like six tiny, shining six-sided feathers – and this . . .'

'Grandpa, it's like magic!' said Dick. 'I never knew that snow was made up of tiny crystals, all six-sided, all different.'

'And all beautiful!' said Grandpa. 'Ah, there are plenty of things like this in the world, if you have eyes to see them. Well, Susan, do you think you can go back to your pattern-making now, and make designs like my friend, Mr Frost?'

'Oh, you mean *Jack* Frost, of course!' said Susan with a laugh. 'Well, I must say I never thought of him as a designer of patterns before. I'm going straight indoors to put down some of his glorious designs!'

She drew some beautiful six-sided ones, and signed her name at the bottom. After her name she added a few words that made Grandpa smile. This is what she put: *Drawn with the kind help of Mr Jack Frost.*

IT'S LIKE MAGIC!

Did *you* know about the six-sided crystals that make up the soft, light snowflakes? See if you can buy or borrow a magnifying glass and a bit of black cloth, and then go out in the snow to see them. I'd like to hear about it if you do!

The Domino Brownie

The Domino Brownie

ONCE THERE was a brownie called Twinkles who worked for Santa Claus in his castle. There were a great many little folk there, working hard all the year round to get thousands of toys ready for old Santa to put in his enormous sack at Christmas time. Twinkles had one special job to do – and that was to paint the spots on the dominoes.

He was very good at this. He had pots of all kinds of different colours, and he carried his paintbrushes in a leather holder fastened to his belt. He painted blue spots on yellow dominoes, red spots on black ones, orange spots on brown ones, and, of course, did a great many black-spotted dominoes too.

But one day he got a bit bored with his dominoes. He had done three hundred and sixty-four that day, and he was tired of it. He looked around for a bit of mischief and saw quite near to him the three gnomes Snippy, Snappy and Snorum bending over a doll's house, neat and clean in their white overalls.

I'll paint them like dominoes! thought Twinkles, and in a trice he had painted double-three on Snippy, five-four on Snappy and double-six on Snorum! How funny their backs looked to be sure!

Twinkles began to giggle. He looked round for something else to do, and he caught sight of the big plain doors. He would make them all into big dominoes!

So, while the other workers were at dinner, Twinkles made four doors into dominoes! One door was two-three, another was five-one, the third was double-four and the last was blank-two! Naughty Twinkles! The doors did look funny!

And then he saw some dolls waiting for their faces to be painted in – and in a trice Twinkles had given them domino faces. How strange they looked! Twinkles chuckled – and then he stood still in a fright. He had heard the voice of Santa Claus, who just happened to be paying a flying visit that afternoon!

'Now, what's all this, what's all this?' came his big, booming voice. 'Here are my doors all staring at me like dominoes – and you gnomes seem to have domino overalls – and, bless us all, if the dolls haven't got domino faces too!

'This won't do, this won't do!' said Santa, picking up a doll whose face was a double-five. 'What do you suppose the children will say if I gave them dolls with faces like this? WHO DID IT?'

'I d-d-d-did,' stammered Twinkles.

'Well, finish your job and take a week's notice,' said Santa. 'Can't have anyone playing about like this with children's toys!'

Poor Twinkles! He finished his work and then, at

the end of the week, he saw another domino brownie coming to do his dominoes. Sadly he picked up the only pot of paint he had over, and left the castle.

He came to our world and for a long time he wandered about, asking if he might paint dominoes on different things. He wanted to paint domino spots on a tortoise's shell and on birds' eggs and on snails – but not a single creature would let him. At last he found one that said yes, he would like domino spots to make him pretty – so what do you think he does now? Guess! He paints the black spots on the red backs of the little ladybirds! Look at them – they are like tiny, curved dominoes. I hope you catch Twinkles at work one day – wouldn't it be fun?

The Brownie's Spectacles

The Brownie's Spectacles

THERE WAS once a small boy called Billy. He had four brothers and sisters, and all the children lived with their mother and father in a tiny cottage. Their parents were very poor, and Billy could not remember a single Christmas time when any stocking had been filled, or any birthday when there had been a birthday cake.

The cottage was at the edge of a wood, and the children were forbidden to go there. 'It is said that there are brownies and gnomes living in the wood,' said their father. 'It is best not to go among the trees, for the little folk might take you to work for them.'

But Billy did not think the brownies were unkind. He had seen one or two, and he thought their faces were as kind as his father's and mother's. But he was an obedient boy, so he did not go into the wood.

One day he was searching for firewood at the edge of the trees. He had a sack that he was filling with twigs and branches. His mother used the wood for the fire, and it was Billy's job to bring in a sackful each day. He picked up twigs busily, and then stopped to listen. Surely he could hear something?

Yes, he could. It was the sound of someone saying, 'Oh, dear, oh, dear, oh, dear!' over and over again! Who could it be?

He soon found out. Behind a tree sat a small brownie with a very sad face, and it was he who was saying, 'Oh, dear!' so many times.

'Hallo!' said Billy, coming up. 'What's the matter?'

The brownie jumped in fright. 'Oh, I didn't hear you coming!' he said. 'Look! I've broken my spectacles!'

Billy looked on the ground. There were the

brownie's spectacles smashed to pieces! There was no mending them at all.

'I dropped them off my nose,' said the brownie sorrowfully, 'and as I am quite blind without them I can't walk another step. So here I must stay until my brother, Longbeard, comes by late this evening. And I have my dinner cooking away in my cottage, and my old grandmother coming to tea. Oh, dear, oh, dear, oh, dear, oh, dear! Oh ...'

'I've never heard so many "Oh, dears" in my life,' said Billy, laughing. 'Cheer up! If you'll tell me the way, I'll take you to your cottage. Then you will be able to see to your dinner and give your grandmother tea when she comes.'

'Now, that *is* kind of you!' said the brownie gratefully. 'I've another pair of glasses at home, so I shall be all right once I get there. Give me your arm, little boy, and I'll tell you the way to go. Go round the big oak tree to start with – and then between the tall bracken – and then ...'

Billy guided the little fellow the way he said, and it wasn't long before they arrived at a small blue house set under a great big tree. It had a very large garden indeed, set with tiny trees and nothing else. Not a single flower grew in it.

'Thanks very much indeed,' said the brownie, opening the door of the cottage. 'Could you look on this top shelf for me and see if my other pair of glasses are there?'

Billy found them, and the brownie put them on his nose. 'Ah!' he said, delighted. 'Now I can see again! Good! Now what about a glass of lemonade?'

'I'd love one,' said Billy, 'but I'm afraid I mustn't stay. My mother is waiting for her firewood.'

'Wait a moment,' said the brownie. 'I'd just like to give you a present for your kindness.'

He ran out of the back door. Billy waited, feeling most excited. A brownie present might be something really wonderful – a sack of gold, a magic purse, a beautiful jewel!

But it wasn't any of those. The brownie came back carrying a small tree that he had just dug out of his garden. It was a tiny fir tree.

'Here you are,' he said. 'It's a little Christmas tree. You may find it useful. It's the only thing I can give you.'

Billy was dreadfully disappointed. Only a baby fir tree, the kind he could dig up himself in the wood any day! But he was a polite little boy and he thanked the brownie, said goodbye and ran off.

When he got home he told his mother of the brownie. She looked at the tree.

'You are foolish, Billy,' she said. 'You should have asked him for something else. Those brownies know a lot of magic. He might have done you some good. Throw this silly little tree away.'

'Oh, I'll plant it in my garden,' said Billy. 'It's a dear little tree. I may as well keep it.'

So he planted it in his garden and then forgot all about it. The summer passed and autumn came. The little tree grew well. Then the autumn passed into cold winter, and the frost and snow came. The little cottage was cold, for the children could not find enough wood to keep a good fire going. There was not enough to eat either, and when Christmas time came near, Billy knew it was no use hanging up stockings.

'Father Christmas can't know where we live,' he told the others, 'and Mother and Father are too poor to buy any presents for us. We must just pretend!'

'Dig up your little tree and let us pretend it is covered with all sorts of presents,' said one of the little girls.

So Billy went out and dug up the tree. He put it into a little tub and stood it on the table in the kitchen.

'There you are!' he said to the children. 'There's our Christmas tree! We shall have to pretend there are toys on it!'

'There shall be a big doll for me!' cried one little girl.

'And a big book of stories for me!' cried the other.

'A train for me!' shouted Billy's brother.

'*Gug-gug-gug*!' said the baby, which meant all kinds of things.

'A fat purse for Mother!' said Billy. 'And a good pipe and tobacco for Father! And a box of money for me!'

But it was only pretending. There was nothing on the little tree at all. It was very sad.

'Tomorrow is Christmas Eve,' said Billy. 'I wish Father Christmas would fill our stockings, but I know he won't. Besides, only Baby has stockings this Christmas. We haven't any.'

The next night the little tree was put in the scullery out of the way – but when Billy went to wash he looked at the tree in surprise. Buds were growing at the end of each little branch. How strange at this time of year! He looked at it carefully. There was no mistaking it – there *were* buds!

He carried the tree into the kitchen and set it on the

table. 'Look, Mother,' he said, 'this little tree seems to be budding. Isn't it funny?'

Everyone looked – and, do you know, even as they stared at the tree, they could see the buds growing. Yes, really, they were getting bigger each minute!

Then one of the buds burst – and what do you suppose its flower was? Guess!

It was a little red candle! Wasn't that curious? Then another bud burst – and yet another – and they all flowered into candles!

'See this very fat bud!' said Billy in great excitement. 'Whatever can it be going to burst into?'

It certainly was very fat, and it went on growing and growing. It burst at last – and guess what it was! A big doll with curly golden hair, blue eyes and a pink silk dress! There it hung on the tree, like a big pink blossom. It was the most wonderful and surprising thing that the children had ever seen.

'Mother! It's a magic tree!' cried Billy. 'Oh, how glad I am that I didn't throw it away! Just look at it!

It's full of buds! I do wonder what they will all be!'

You should have seen that Christmas tree. It was really a wonderful sight. Its buds burst one after another into the loveliest things. There was a train, a book of stories, a pipe, a purse full of money, a box full of shillings, a shawl, two pairs of boots, a necklace, a box of soldiers, a pink rabbit, a blue pig and heaps of other things! The children cut the strange toy flowers off, and as fast as they cut them off more buds grew, burst and became toys or other presents.

'What a wonderful tree!' cried everyone. 'We shall have a fine Christmas now!'

'I'm going out to spend some of my money,' said Billy. 'I'm going to buy a fat goose for tomorrow's dinner, and a Christmas pudding, and lots of sausages, cakes, biscuits and fruit! Hurray! This will be our first good Christmas!'

Well, it certainly *was* a good Christmas! The little magic tree went on flowering until midnight, and then it stopped – but, dear me, by that time the cottage was quite crammed with good things! It looked as if Father Christmas had emptied twenty sacks there!

'Tomorrow morning I am going to see that brownie who broke his spectacles and thank him very much,' said Billy. 'I didn't know the tree was such a marvellous one.'

So the next day he set off to the little blue cottage. When he got there what a sight met his eyes! All the little fir trees in the brownie's garden had flowered in the night, and the ground was covered with all kinds of lovely things. The brownie was busy picking them up and putting them into sacks.

'Hallo!' he said to Billy. 'I hope your tree flowered all right.'

'Oh, yes, and I've come to say "Thank you very much indeed",' said Billy. 'I didn't know it was Christmas trees you grew. I thought it was ordinary trees.'

'Dear me, no,' said the brownie. 'I grow these for Father Christmas. He took about five hundred from me this Christmas. The rest have all flowered, as you see. I am gathering up the toys to send away to children's parties.'

'Will my tree flower again next year?' asked Billy.

'Of course!' said the brownie. 'It has a Christmas spell in it, you know.'

'Oh, how lovely!' said Billy. 'I *am* glad I found you when you broke your spectacles that day in the summer, brownie! If you hadn't we wouldn't have had our lovely tree, and all our presents, and our Christmas goose and Christmas pudding and everything! We are *so* happy!'

Off he went – and you can guess what a lovely time he and his brothers and sisters had that Christmas Day. The little tree has been carefully planted in Billy's garden again. He will dig it up next Christmas Eve. Wouldn't you like to see it flowering into toys? I would!

Santa Claus Makes
a Mistake

Santa Claus Makes
a Mistake

ELLEN AND Jack were very excited. It was Christmas Eve, and they meant to hang up their stockings at the end of their beds. Daddy had given each of them one of his big ones, and they were very pleased.

They hung them up and then jumped into bed. 'You must go to sleep quickly,' Mother said, 'because, you know, Santa Claus won't come until you are fast asleep.'

So Ellen and Jack shut their eyes and tried to go to sleep – and it wasn't very long before they were both fast asleep and dreaming. They slept and slept, while the clock struck eight – and nine, and ten, and eleven! All the grown-ups went to bed. The lights were turned out. The house was dark.

The dog slept on his rug. The cat slept in her basket. Everything was quiet – except the fire in the dining room, which made a little noise now and again when the hot coals fell together.

Towards midnight Ellen woke up suddenly. She sat up in bed, wondering what had awakened her. The nursery was dark. Jack was fast asleep. She could hear him breathing.

She listened. She thought perhaps she might have been dreaming. She switched on the light and looked around the nursery. She looked at the end of the bed where she and Jack had hung their stockings. To her great disappointment they were quite empty.

'I wonder if that is because Santa Claus hasn't been yet,' wondered Ellen. 'Oh, how dreadful it will be if we find our stockings empty in the morning!'

Just as she was turning out the light she heard the noise again. It was a funny noise – a sort of scraping, kicking noise – and then she heard a deep groan.

Goodness gracious, whatever can it be! thought Ellen. She leant over to Jack's bed and woke him up.

The scraping noise went on and on. Jack sat up and asked Ellen what all the noise was about.

'Jack,' said Ellen, 'I can't help thinking it's someone stuck in the chimney downstairs! That's what it sounds like to me. Oh, Jack, do you suppose it's Santa Claus?'

'I say!' said Jack. 'I say! Suppose it is! Suppose he's stuck! Come on quickly, Ellen, we must go and see.'

The two children put on their dressing gowns and slippers, pushed open their door and slipped down the stairs. They went into the dining room and saw the little red fire there. They heard the dog growling in the kitchen, for he too had heard the strange noises.

'Look! Look!' said Ellen, pointing to the fireplace. 'There's a boot hanging down the chimney! Look!'

Sure enough, there was a boot there – a big black boot – and it was on a leg, and the leg was kicking about! As the children watched, another boot came down the chimney.

'It *is* Santa Claus!' said Jack. 'He always wears big black boots in his pictures. Oh, Ellen, he's come down the wrong chimney. He'll burn himself on the fire!'

'I'll put it out before he does,' said Ellen at once. She turned on the light and went to the kitchen. She filled a jug at the tap and carried it back to the dining room. She poured the water on the fire.

Sizzle-sizzle-sizzle! The fire streamed up in a cloud of thick black smoke! A startled voice from the chimney said, 'Hallo! Is anybody there? My word, this smoke is going to make me sneeze!'

'It's only Ellen and Jack,' said Jack. 'We know you are Santa Claus. We've put the fire out so that you won't get burnt. That is why it is smoking so much. We've just poured some water on it. You've come down the wrong chimney, Santa Claus.'

'Dear, dear!' said Santa Claus. 'Have I really? You know, I have a map showing the chimneys of every house, and the right ones, leading to the children's bedrooms, are marked with a yellow cross – and tonight the wind blew my map away so I had to guess! And I've guessed wrong! I'm stuck here.'

'We could give you a pull,' said Ellen. 'Jack can take one leg and I can pull the other.'

'Go on then,' said Santa Claus.

So they each took hold of a black-booted leg and pulled hard. Santa Claus came down with a rush and sat in the fire-place! – a big burly man in red, with a twinkling smile and the kindest eyes the children had ever seen.

'These coals are still hot!' said Santa Claus, getting up in a hurry. 'It's kind of you children to help me like this. Do you mind if I stay here for a little while till the reindeer I sent to look for my blown-away map comes back and gives it to me? I shall most likely make a few more mistakes if I go on guessing which are the right chimneys.'

'Oh, Santa Claus, of course stay as long as you

like,' said Ellen. 'We'd simply love you to. I'll get some of my chocolates for you.'

'You don't suppose the grown-ups will wake up and hear me, do you?' whispered Santa Claus, suddenly remembering that there were other people in the house. 'I never know what to say to grown-ups, you know. They make me shy. It's children I like.'

'Oh, I don't think Mummy and Daddy will wake,' said Ellen. 'They sleep very soundly. And Cook and Jane sleep at the top of the house. The only thing that might happen is that Spot, our dog, may bark.'

'Well, go and bring him here,' said Santa Claus. 'I have a rubber bone for him, I think. It was down on my list – one dog, one rubber bone – and he might as well have it now. Dogs don't seem to hang stockings up, so I usually give them a present straight away or put it into their baskets if they are not awake.'

Jack went to fetch Spot, who seemed most delighted to see Santa Claus. He jumped up on his knee and licked his face all over.

'His tongue is as good as a sponge!' said Santa Claus. 'Here, Spot, lick this bone for a change. I really don't think my face wants washing any more.'

Jack and Ellen were so happy. It was the greatest adventure in the world to be sitting with Santa Claus, hearing him talk and laugh, and seeing him eat their chocolates.

Suddenly there came a little soft knocking at the window. Santa Claus jumped up. 'That's my reindeer come back!' he said.

He opened the window softly – and, to the children's enormous surprise, a big furry head was pushed in! It was the head of one of the reindeer. Its antlers were so big that they could not get inside the window, so the reindeer could only put in its big soft nose, so long and velvety. In its mouth it held a large piece of paper.

'Thanks, reindeer,' said Santa Claus, and he rubbed its nose. 'I'm glad to get my map back again. Have you got a bit of sugar for the old fellow, children?'

'Of course!' said Ellen, and she ran to the sideboard where the basin of sugar was kept. She took out a handful of sugar-lumps and she and Jack fed the delighted reindeer. Then Santa Claus shut the window and looked at the map. It was a most curious map, showing nothing but chimneys, and the page was marked with scores of yellow crosses.

'Well, my dears,' said Santa Claus with a sigh, rolling up his map, 'I must be off! I have so much enjoyed this little time with you – nice kind creatures children are! I always did like them much better than grown-ups. I'm a bit late now, because of losing this map, so I must be off. Thanks so much for your help, and the chocolates, and the sugar-lumps. Do you mind letting me out of the front door? I don't like to try that chimney again, you know.'

The children took Santa Claus to the front door and let him out. He gave them each a hug and disappeared into the night. They heard him whistling to his reindeer, and listened to the jingling of the sleigh bells as the reindeer moved up to Santa Claus.

Ellen and Jack shut the door and went up to bed. They were so excited that they could not go to sleep.

'I'm afraid we shan't have any presents in our stockings, Ellen,' said Jack. 'Santa Claus won't come here now.'

'Well, I don't mind,' said Ellen. 'I've *seen* him, and spoken to him, and fed his reindeer and given him a hug! I don't care if he never fills my stockings again! He's real, and I've seen him!'

It was a long time before the children did at last fall asleep. And, you know, in the morning when they sat up in bed their stockings were fuller than they had ever been before! And there were presents on the bed and on the floor too!

'He *did* come back again!' said Ellen in delight. 'Oh, the darling! Look what's in our stockings, Jack – the loveliest toys we've ever had!'

'Now don't say a word to anyone about us seeing Santa Claus last night and pulling him down the chimney,' said Jack. 'He'd like us to keep it a secret, I know. Fancy him coming back again to our house – and getting the chimney right this time!'

Daddy and Mummy were *so* surprised to see what a lot of things the children had in their stockings and on the bed. 'It was a good thing you were asleep when he came,' said Mummy. 'He doesn't like children to see him, you know.'

She couldn't *think* why Ellen and Jack looked at one another and smiled when she said that – but I know why, don't you?

The Children Who Weren't Asked

The Children Who Weren't Asked

JOHNNIE AND Susie Morrison always had a wonderful party just after Christmas. They were twins and their birthdays came then, so their mother put Christmas and birthdays together and gave them a really lovely party!

Johnnie and Susie always enjoyed their party tremendously – but the other children enjoyed it even more! It began at three and lasted till seven, and there was always a fine conjuror and a treasure hunt too.

Alice and Peter Collins loved the Morrisons' party almost more than anyone else, because they didn't go to many. They thought the Morrisons' party was just as good as Christmas!

'We shall soon get our invitation,' said Alice. 'I know the date – it's the date of the twins' birthday, December 29th. I'm glad I've got a new frock.'

The invitations didn't seem to come as early as they usually did. Christmas came and went, and still no invitation card had come.

'They're leaving it rather late!' said Peter. 'But I know they're having the party as usual, because Mrs Mills, the baker's wife, told me she is making some special chocolate cakes for it.'

'Oooh!' said Alice. 'I can't wait for the day!'

When they went out that morning they saw Joan ahead of them. She called out to a boy across the road. 'Are you going to the Morrisons' party?'

'Rather!' he said. 'I've answered my invitation already.'

Alice and Peter looked at one another, and felt rather sick. So the invitations *had* gone out then! And they hadn't had one.

They went home feeling miserable. 'We've been left out,' said Alice. 'I wonder why?'

'It's funny,' said Peter. 'We've been three times before. Oh, dear, it's so very horrid to be left out, isn't it, Alice? The other children are sure to ask us if we are going.'

'Well, we must just say "No, we're sorry we're not",' said Alice.

So when Gladys and Roy and Winnie and Sam met them in the next two or three days, and asked the same question, 'Are you going to the Morrisons' party?', Alice and Peter said what they had planned to say, 'No. We're sorry we're not!'

'It will be awkward if we meet Johnnie or Susie,' said Alice. 'I don't feel as if I like them much now. I hate being left out like this.'

'Well, if we see them we'll cross over or turn down a corner or something,' said Peter. So, whenever they saw the twins in the distance they were careful not to go near them.

Alice worried and worried about it. Had she or Peter done anything the twins didn't like? Did Mrs Morrison think their manners weren't good enough? Didn't the twins like them any more?

Peter wasn't so worried, but he thought it was mean. Every other child in the village seemed to be going to the party. It looked dreadful for them to be left out. Luckily his mother hadn't seemed to realise it, so that was all right. It would have worried her too, because she was proud of Alice and Peter.

Every morning Alice hoped secretly that the invitation would come. It might have been delayed perhaps. It would turn up after all!

But it didn't. The day of the party came and still there was no invitation card. Peter looked at Alice gloomily.

'It won't be very pleasant seeing all the others going by to the party this afternoon, will it?' he said.

'No,' said Alice, nearly crying. 'And it will be *horrid* at school next week hearing them all talk about it, and we shan't be able to say a word. Oh, I do hate those twins.'

'So do I,' said Peter. 'It's such a mean trick just to leave us two out. Nobody else has been left out at all.'

They went out to the shops for their mother. On the way back they saw a little dog trotting in front of them. It was the twins' cocker spaniel out on his own.

He ran across the road and a bicycle came round the corner. It ran straight into the little dog, and the rider almost fell off. He shouted at the frightened dog and rode away.

The dog limped to the kerb. It lay down. It whined pitifully and licked its paws.

'It's hurt,' said Alice. 'Oh, Peter!'

'*Let* it be hurt,' said Peter. 'It's the twins' dog, and it's probably as horrid as they are.'

'Oh, Peter — it's a dear little dog,' said Alice. 'We *must* see to it. We must. You can't be as horrid as you sound!'

Peter wasn't, of course. He was really a very

kind-hearted boy, and he went with Alice at once to see to the dog. The dog knew them and whined. Peter picked it up and carried it to his home.

He and Alice bathed the crushed paw and bandaged it. They gave the dog some warm milk and fussed over it. It licked them and wagged its tail.

'It's all right now,' said Peter. 'But I don't know if it can walk. That front paw is really hurt and this back one looks very sore.'

The dog tried to walk, but it couldn't. It rolled over and looked helplessly up at the children, as if to say 'Sorry! But I just can't walk.'

'We can't possibly carry it to the Morrisons' door,' said Peter. 'I never want to go into their gate again! We'll take it to the gate and push it just inside. Then the Morrisons will find it, or hear it whining. I just won't speak to that horrid, unkind family.'

So they took turns in carrying the spaniel to the Morrisons' gate. But Alice was really too kind-hearted to push it inside and leave it. 'I can't,' she said. 'I'll just *have* to take it to the house. I don't care – if I have to speak to those horrid twins, well, it just can't be helped. It's for the dog's sake after all.'

They marched up to the front door and rang the bell. The door soon opened and there stood Mrs Morrison, smiling at them.

'Oh, has something happened to Scamper?' she said. 'You *are* kind children to bring him back, and you've bandaged his paw, I see. The twins *will* be grateful to you.'

She took the dog and turned to call the twins.

'Come on,' said Peter in a low voice. 'We don't need to stop now.'

So they went down the path. Mrs Morrison turned and saw them. 'I'll be seeing you this afternoon at the party!' she called. 'I'll thank you properly then, my dears.'

They turned at once. 'But we haven't been *asked*,' said Alice. 'Have you forgotten?'

Mrs Morrison stared in surprise. 'Don't be silly,

Alice dear,' she said. 'Of course you and Peter have been asked. Why, your names were among the first to be put down on our list. Do you mean to say you didn't get your invitation?'

'No. We haven't had one,' said Peter.

'Well, how strange!' said Mrs Morrison. 'You *will* come though, won't you? Why, we've got presents for you and everything! The twins wondered why you hadn't answered. Well, you *must* have thought it strange if you didn't get an invitation like all the others!'

Peter went rather red. Alice looked suddenly excited. 'Can we really come?' she said. 'You *did* mean us to? Oh, Mrs Morrison, how lovely! We did so want to come!'

'Yes, of course you must come,' said kind Mrs Morrison. 'Three o'clock. And thank you *so* much for looking after our little dog. That just shows what nice children you are, to bring back the dog when you thought we'd left you out!'

The two children rushed off, excited and happy.

It was all a mistake! They were to go. They hadn't been left out after all. What a very good thing they had taken Scamper back to the house!

And now I expect you wonder why they hadn't had an invitation. Well, the twins explained it all that afternoon.

'You see, Mummy put all the invitations into my doll's pram for me to take to the post,' said Susie. 'And one slipped under the pillow – yours! We've just found it there. So it wasn't posted. I'm so sorry. But it doesn't matter now you're here.'

No, it didn't matter. Everything was lovely again. Mrs Morrison was kind, the twins were as jolly as ever, and the party was twice as good as usual.

As for the spaniel he had a new red bow and was made such a fuss of because of his bad leg that he really enjoyed the party more than anyone!

One Christmas Night

One Christmas Night

THREE CHILDREN sat in a caravan on Christmas Eve – a boy and two girls, Tom, Polly and Sue. They crouched over a small oil-stove and shivered.

'I hope Mummy won't be long,' said Sue, the smallest. 'I hope she'll bring back lots of nice things from the shops.'

'Well, she won't,' said Tom. 'She's got hardly any money left. She told me so. It took quite a lot to move from our house into this caravan.'

'I don't like the caravan,' said Polly. 'It's so small. I didn't like leaving our little house today and moving here.'

'Well, we'll only be here till Daddy comes out of hospital and goes back to work again,' said Tom. 'We've got to put up with it – so don't let's upset Mummy by grumbling all the time.'

'It's Christmas tomorrow,' said Sue. 'Last year we had a little tree, and a plum pudding, and our stockings had presents in them. Will Mummy bring some presents back?'

'No,' she won't,' said Tom.

'Well, perhaps Father Christmas will come tonight,' said Sue. 'He's got plenty of toys in his sack, hasn't he?'

'Tom,' said Polly suddenly, 'our caravan hasn't any chimney. Did you know? So Santa Claus can't possibly climb down to fill our stockings.'

Sue began to cry. She was only six, and everything seemed topsy-turvy and strange to her the last few days. Daddy had gone away ill. Mummy had found this caravan to live in because it was cheap. Now it seemed as if they weren't going to have any

Christmas at all – not even stockings!

'Don't cry, Sue,' said Tom. 'You'll only make Mummy unhappy, and she's very worried already. Polly, can't we do something to help a bit? What about that pile of clothes over there? Couldn't we wash them for her?'

'Yes, we could,' said Polly, getting up. 'Mummy will be tired when she gets back. Get some water from the stream, Tom – there's the pail. We'll heat it over the top of the stove.'

But when the water was warm enough to wash in, Polly found that there was hardly any soap! 'Oh, well, I'll wash out the *little* things,' she said. 'The hankies, and this collar, and our stockings and socks. Tom, go and put up a little line for me from the caravan to that tree, will you?'

So, when Mummy came back, there was a little line of washing hanging out, and she was so pleased to think that the children had tried to do something for her.

She made tea in the little caravan, and told them about the shops and how gay they looked. Sue hardly listened and her mother wondered why she looked so miserable. 'What's the matter, Sue?' she asked. 'Cheer up! You'll soon get used to this nice little caravan.'

'It isn't nice,' said Sue. 'It hasn't got a chimney – so Father Christmas can't climb down and fill our stockings!'

'Well, never mind – we'll have to miss out that kind of thing this year,' said Mummy. 'We'll just have to pretend it isn't Christmas at all – except that I really must tell you the story of the first Christmas night, as I always do.'

She told them the story of little Jesus born in a stable and laid in a manger for a cradle – and how the sky was full of angels singing joyfully that night. Then she put Sue and Polly to bed. Tom stayed up a little while, trying to be as grown-up as he could, and make up to his mother for his father being away in hospital.

He went to bed at last and his mother lay down on a mattress spread on the floor. The caravan was in darkness.

They were all fast asleep when a noise awoke Tom. He sat up. Whatever was it? Something seemed to be on the roof of the caravan! There was a scraping noise – and then a loud exclamation. 'It's fallen off the roof! What a thing to happen!'

Tom's heart began to beat fast. He didn't dare to move. He heard footsteps on the roof and then someone seemed to jump down from it to the ground. He heard the soft jingle of bells from somewhere too. It couldn't be Father Christmas surely!

Tom sat and listened to the noises. Polly awoke too, and he whispered to her what was happening. 'Don't wake Mummy – she's so tired,' he said. 'Shall we go and see what's happening?'

They took a torch and crept out of the caravan door, stepping carefully over their sleeping mother. The first thing they saw in the silent darkness, lit by their torch, was a large sack!

It had burst open at the neck – and toys were falling out! Dolls, engines, ships, soldiers – good gracious!

'Are they for us? Has Father Christmas left them here for us three children?' said Polly in delight.

Tom stared at the open sack. He shook his head. 'No. Do you know what I think happened? Father Christmas landed on our roof – couldn't see a chimney – and dropped his sack off the roof while he was looking for one.'

'Well, why did he leave it here?' asked Polly. 'Won't he want it to fill other children's stockings?'

'Yes, of course – but do you know what he's done? He's taken our big sack of potatoes instead!' said Tom. 'Mummy put it there, in that corner, so that we could easily get potatoes from it – and it's gone. Father Christmas must have picked it up in his hurry, and gone off with it, thinking it was his sack of toys!'

'Goodness!' said Polly, and she picked up a doll.

'Well, let's help ourselves, Tom. My word, we'll have plenty of toys now!'

'Polly! They're not ours,' said Tom, shocked. 'Father Christmas will be sure to come back for them. I'm going to tie up the neck of the sack, drag it out over there and light a lantern to put on the top of it. Then he'll see it when he comes back to look for it!'

'Oh, well, I suppose you're right,' said Polly, bitterly disappointed. 'Can we stay out and watch for him?'

'No. It's freezing cold,' said Tom. 'We're shivering already! Get back into the caravan. I'll drag the sack into the open and light the old lantern.'

Tom soon had the sack tied up, dragged it into a clear space, and put the lit lantern on the top. There, now Father Christmas would see it easily. What a pity he didn't know there were children in the caravan without a chimney just nearby! How Sue would have loved a little doll – and Polly too.

He went back to the caravan. Polly was asleep again

already. Tom tried to keep awake to hear Father Christmas coming back – but his eyes closed and he was soon dreaming.

He didn't hear the soft jingling of bells. He didn't hear someone outside the caravan – someone who put back the sack of potatoes and picked up the sack of toys to put into his sleigh. The lantern was blown out and set down beside the potatoes – and then bells jingled softly again, fading away in the distance.

Tom and Polly remembered what had happened in the night as soon as they awoke. They told their mother and Sue. Mummy laughed. 'You dreamt it all! If Father Christmas had really come, he would have popped some toys through the window for you!'

'It was shut,' said Tom. 'And the door was locked. And there's no chimney. But he *did* come – Polly and I saw the sack of toys all burst open.'

'I want a toy!' wailed Sue suddenly. 'It's Christmas morning. I want a toy!'

'Wipe your eyes, Sue, and stop crying,' said

Mummy. 'Where's your hanky?'

'I washed it. It's out on the line,' said Polly. 'I'll go and fetch it for Sue.'

Out she went – and in a second or two she was back, her face red and her eyes shining. 'Mummy! Tom! Sue! Come and look! Oh, DO come and look! You'll hardly believe your eyes!'

They all went out of the caravan. Polly pointed to the little washing line that Tom had put up. On it were the things that Polly had washed – a collar, hankies, and stockings and socks belonging to them all.

'Look! Every sock, every stocking on the line has got something in it!' cried Polly. 'Sue, this sock of yours is full of sweets – and this one has a doll! Tom, this stocking of yours has an engine – feel! Mummy, your stockings have got something in too! Look! Oh, isn't it wonderful?'

Polly was right. Every sock and stocking was filled with something – and, will you believe it, there was a little purse full of money for Mummy! She could hardly believe her eyes.

Polly had a doll, a book, a tiny workbox, sweets and all kinds of things. Sue had a whole crowd of little farm animals besides her doll – and, as for Tom, he had just the things he wanted!

There was a tiny note in one stocking. Mummy read it out loud.

'Thanks very much for leaving my sack lit up for me. I saw the socks and stockings on the line in the light of the lantern – so I guessed there were children in the caravan, though there was no chimney for me to climb down and see how many. So I've filled all the socks and stockings there are.

'Happy Christmas from your loving

F. C.'

'Mummy! We *told* you it was true that he came last

night!' said Polly. 'Oh, Mummy, *what* a good thing I did that bit of washing for you yesterday and hung it on the line! If I hadn't, Father Christmas would never have known there were children in the caravan.'

They had a wonderful Christmas after all. The caravan was warm and cheerful, and all the toys made a splendid show. Best of all there was plenty of money in Mummy's little purse to buy lots of lovely things when Christmas was over.

And now Polly has a message to send to all children whose homes have no chimney – 'just hang up a few stockings on your washing line – and see what's there in the morning!'

The New Year's Imp

The New Year's Imp

DIANA AND Keith had a lovely Christmas. They had a stocking full of toys, crackers, a plum pudding with money in, and a fine Christmas tree decked with brightly burning candles.

And the presents they had!

Diana had a toy sewing-machine from Auntie Winnie, a new doll from her mother, a book from her father, skittles from Uncle Ned, a pair of stockings from Auntie Lou, a picture for her bedroom from Mrs Peterson down the road, a pair of snow boots from her granny and a sledge from her grandpa! What lovely presents!

Keith had just as many, and the two children had spent a happy time on Christmas morning opening them all, then exclaiming over them.

'Oh, what a lovely engine from Auntie Lou,' said his mother. 'You must write and thank her very nicely, Keith.'

'Yes, Mother,' said Keith, but he didn't mean to. He thought he would wait till he saw Auntie Lou, then he could *say* thank you. It was such a bother to write.

Now this happened every birthday and every Christmas. Diana and Keith put off writing their thanks until their mother had forgotten all about it! It was partly her fault, of course – she should have sat them down with pen and paper the day after Christmas or after their birthday, and told them to write their letters nicely. But all she did was to say 'Don't forget, dears,' so, of course, they forgot!

Now, it is most annoying to spend a lot of time and money going round the shops to buy a really nice present for someone you love, and then never to hear even if they have got it! And you can imagine that every Christmas there are aunts and uncles, grannies and grandpas, and all kinds of friends grumbling very loudly because the children they have remembered haven't even written the smallest letter of thanks!

Their grumbles reached Santa Claus, and disturbed him as he rested after his heavy work on Christmas Eve. 'Why do these people keep *on* giving presents if they never even hear whether they have been received or not?' he said to his little imps round him.

'They are kind people, but they are foolish,' said a prick-eared imp.

'Well, *I* am kind, but I am not foolish,' said Santa Claus. 'I shall think of a good idea about it. I shall think very hard.'

So he thought, and a good plan grew in his head. He called the prick-eared imp to him.

'Now listen, Prick-Ear,' he said, 'on New Year's Day, you shall take a sack – mine if you like – and go round and collect all those toys that have been given to children who haven't said thank you for them. We'll take them to the hospitals for the sick children, or to poor children who have hardly any toys.'

'Why can't I go now, master?' asked the imp.

'Well, we'll give the children a *chance* to say thank you,' said Santa Claus. 'If you go on New Year's Day, they will have had a week to write or say thank you. That will be fair. I should think my sack will be big enough for the toys you'll collect.'

Well, on New Year's Day the prick-eared imp slipped down the chimney, just as Santa Claus does, and popped into Keith's nursery. Keith and Diana were both there. They stared in astonishment at the business-like imp.

'What do you want?' they said.

'Well, could you find me your sewing-machine, your skittles, your new stockings, your picture, your snow boots and your sledge?' said the imp politely to Diana. 'And could you give me your engine, your aeroplane, your snow boots, your sledge, your new book and your stamp album?' he said to Keith.

'Whatever for?' said Keith.

'Well, you haven't said thank you for them, so I've orders from Santa Claus to collect them and take them to the hospital for children,' said Prick-Ear. 'Sorry and all that – but orders are orders!'

'I never heard of such a thing!' cried Keith in a rage. 'Of course you won't have our new toys. Go away!'

'My orders are that if you don't obey me, I have to empty your toy cupboard completely,' said the imp still politely. 'Sorry and all that.'

'I'll lock the toy cupboard door,' cried Diana, and she did. But the imp didn't mind locked doors a bit. The toy cupboard opened at a touch of his hand, and he began to pile everything into his sack.

The children flew at him, but he looked so fierce that they grew afraid. Diana began to cry. 'I was going to write all my thank-you letters today, I really was!'

'You said that yesterday and the day before and the

day before that,' said the imp. 'You're a storyteller. You just *say* you'll do things, but you don't mean to really – or you'd do them. Now hands off that doll! Sorry and all that!'

'Oh, please!' sobbed Diana. 'Give us another chance. Please do. I do, do promise to say thank you this very day. I'll run down the road to Mrs Petersen, who gave me that picture. I'll go and see Granny and Grandpa and thank them. I'll write a very, very nice letter to—'

'Too late,' said Prick-Ear, shaking everything down in his sack. 'You've had a whole week. Isn't that chance enough to do all you say you'll do? And you haven't done it! No more chances for *you*! Sorry and all that!'

The sack was so full that it wouldn't hold another thing. Prick-Ear had to take it to the hospital straight away and hand in the toys. The matron was most astonished to find a lovely pile of them in the hall of the hospital. She simply could *not* imagine where they had come from.

Prick-Ear went to the next child on his list – a girl called Kate, who was the best writer in her form at school.

'And yet you didn't write even the tiniest letter of thanks!' said the imp, collecting five new dolls, three books and a toy telephone. 'Lazy child! Well, if you want to use this toy telephone, you'll have to go to the children's hospital to use it – for that's where it's going!'

Kate had only a few of her Christmas presents left! She had thanked her father and mother and Granny, who was staying with them, but she simply couldn't be bothered to write her thanks to the people who had sent her presents by post. So those all went into Prick-Ear's sack, and once again the matron of the hospital found another pile of lovely toys waiting for her in the hall.

'Strange!' she said. 'I don't know who to thank for these! How I wish I did!'

Well, on New Year's Day that imp went round to

hundreds and hundreds of children, and I can't tell you how many times he filled his sack! He went to some of my little friends, and to some of your little friends, he went to children we've never heard of, and children in the very next street.

At last the hospital really didn't want any more toys! So Prick-Ear took them to some children he knew who had no toys. They ran to the queer little fellow and held out their arms for them.

But will you believe it, if a child didn't say 'Thank you' Prick-Ear took back the toy at once. Ah, he was a good one at carrying out orders, that imp, and no tears moved him or made him give back toys. He was strict and fair and kind, but he wasn't in the least foolish.

The funny thing was, after he had gone, each child whose presents had been taken, sat down at once to write all their thank-you letters! But that didn't bring their toys back, though they had hoped it would.

Last year was the first year Santa Claus sent out

Prick-Ear. I expect he'll send him out this year again. What will happen if he comes to *you*?

'Aha!' I hear you say. 'He'll go away with an empty sack. I've thanked everyone for *my* presents!'

Have you, really? Well done!

Acknowledgements

All efforts have been made to seek necessary permissions.

The stories in this publication first appeared in the following publications:

'The Dog that Hated Christmas' first appeared in *Enid Blyton's Sunny Stories*, No. 101, 1938.

'The Little Fir Tree' first appeared as 'The Little Fir-Tree' in *The Enid Blyton Nature Readers*, No. 30, published by Macmillan in 1946.

'Julia Saves Up' first appeared in *Enid Blyton's Sunny Stories*, No. 395, 1946.

'Fairy's Love' first appeared in *The Teachers World*, No. 1003, 1923.

'The Cracker Fairies' first appeared as 'The Cracker-Fairies' in *Enid Blyton's Sunny Stories*, No. 153, 1939.

'The Midnight Goblins' first appeared in *Sunny Stories for Little Folks*, No. 21, 1927.

'The Christmas Pony' first appeared in *Enid Blyton's Sunny Stories*, No. 522, 1951.

'The Snowman in Boots' first appeared in *Enid Blyton's Sunny Stories*, No. 525, 1952.

'Nid-Nod's Mistake' first appeared in *The Enid Blyton Nature Readers*, No. 27, published by Macmillan in 1946.

'The Empty Doll's House' first appeared as 'The Empty Dolls' House' in *Enid Blyton's Sunny Stories*, No. 396, 1946.

'Grandpa Twinkle' first appeared in *The Teachers World*, No. 1856, 1938.

'The Stolen Reindeer' first appeared in *The Teachers World*, No. 931, 1922.

'The Grateful Pig' first appeared in *The Teachers World*, No. 1650, 1935.

'They Quite Forgot!' first appeared in *Enid Blyton's Magazine*, No. 1, Vol. 3, 1955.

'Mr Wittle's Snowball' first appeared in *The Teachers World*, No. 1593, 1933.

'Look Out for the Snowman!' first appeared in *Enid Blyton's Sunny Stories*, No. 424, 1948.

'Santa Claus Goes to Mr Pink-Whistle' first appeared in *Enid Blyton's Magazine*, No. 26, Vol. 3, 1955.

'The Boy Who Was Left Out' first appeared in *The Teachers World*, No. 1857, 1938.

'The Little Christmas Tree' first appeared in *The Teachers World*, No. 1490, 1931.

'The Christmas Present' first appeared in *Hello Twins, Little Book No. 4*, published by Brockhampton Press in 1951.

'One Christmas Eve' first appeared in *The Teachers World*, No. 1700, 1935.

'The Strange Christmas Tree' first appeared in *Enid Blyton's Sunny Stories*, No. 103, 1938.

'The Cold Snowman' first appeared as 'The Cold Snow-Man' in *Sunny Stories for Little Folks*, No. 200, 1934.

'It's Like Magic!' first appeared in *Enid Blyton's Magazine*, No. 2, Vol. 7, 1959.

'The Domino Brownie' first appeared in *The Teachers World*, No. 1824, 1938.

'The Brownie's Spectacles' first appeared in *Enid Blyton's Sunny Stories*, No. 7, 1937.

'Santa Claus Makes a Mistake' first appeared in *Enid Blyton's Sunny Stories*, No. 48, 1937.

'The Children Who Weren't Asked' first appeared in *Enid Blyton's Sunny Stories*, No. 473, 1950.

'One Christmas Night' first appeared in *Enid Blyton's Magazine*, No. 21, Vol. 1, 1953.

'The New Year's Imp' first appeared in *Enid Blyton's Sunny Stories*, No. 370, 1945.